The Hunted

Also published in Large Print from G.K. Hall by Wayne D. Overholser:

Red Is the Valley

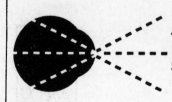

This Large Print Book carries the
Seal of Approval of N.A.V.H.

The Hunted

Wayne D. Overholser

G.K. Hall & Co.
Thorndike, Maine

Copyright © 1965 by Wayne D. Overholser

All rights reserved.

Published in Large Print by arrangement with
Golden West Literary Agency.

G.K. Hall Large Print Book Series.

Printed on acid free paper in Great Britain.

The text of this Large Print edition is unabridged.
Other aspects of the book may vary from the original
edition.

Set in 16 Pt. Plantin.

Library of Congress Cataloging-in-Publication Data

Overholser, Wayne D., 1906–
The hunted: an original novel / Wayne D. Overholser.
    p. cm.
   Originally published under the pseudonym John S.
Daniels.
   ISBN 0-8161-5922-X (alk. paper : lg. print)
   1. Large type books.   I. Title.
[PS3529.V33H86 1994]   94–8807
813'.54—dc20   CIP

CHAPTER ONE

Morgan Dillard dismounted and tied in front of the Harmony State Bank after making the long ride across the Catclaws from his Rafter D on Peace Creek. He glanced at his watch as he stepped up on the boardwalk. It was five minutes until closing time.

For a moment Morgan had a terrible feeling that if his watch was off five minutes he would have made the ride for nothing. He was relieved when he tried the front door of the bank and found that it wasn't locked. He unbuttoned his sheepskin as he went inside. This was almost the end of April. The calendar said it was spring, but the idea was fiction, for spring had not come to either side of the mountains. A cold wind was blowing when he'd left the Rafter D, and it was blowing just as hard over here on Smoky River.

'Damn it, shut the door,' Bud Lamm bellowed from his desk behind the teller's cage.

'Sorry.' Morgan shut the door and crossed to the teller's window. 'I'd like to see your father.'

Bud Lamm had gone to work in the bank the year after he was graduated from high school, two years ago. He had never worked

1

at anything else, and the only reason he had a job here was because his father, Kirk Lamm, owned the bank.

Every time Morgan had been in the bank in the last two years, he'd had to struggle to keep from poking Bud in the nose. The arrogant Lamm manner was hard enough to take from Kirk Lamm; it was doubly hard to take from Bud.

Bud rose and walked to the counter. He stood there a full minute, looking Morgan over from the top of his dusty Stetson to the worn boots, then he asked insolently, 'What for?'

Morgan clenched his fists and fought his temper. Finally he said, 'I'll explain my business to your father.'

Still Bud stood there, a finger of his right hand rubbing a pimple on his chin. Finally he said, 'I'll see if he has time to talk to you.'

He turned and slouched into Kirk Lamm's office in the back. When he came back a moment later, he said, 'He'll see you after awhile.' He returned to his desk and sat down.

Morgan walked to a window and stared across the street at the Belle Union. He saw Doc Vance run out of the saloon and hurry down the street, his derby cocked at a jaunty angle on his head, his black bag in his hand. A baby was on the way, Morgan thought, and the doctor had lingered in the saloon longer than he should have.

A moment later Sheriff Frank Nolan and Orlando Craig who owned the Mercantile left the Belle Union, Nolan swaggering a little, Craig with a fat cigar in his mouth. It was a wonder Kirk Lamm wasn't with them. These three, with Doc Vance, were the big four in Harmony, and in the county, too. Morgan never quite understood how they did it, but somehow they managed to make a profit of almost everything that happened, which usually meant that someone else lost.

Morgan stiffened, his temper, already honed to a fine edge, now almost out of control. Kirk Lamm had just followed the others out of the saloon. He said something to the sheriff and Craig, then crossed the street to the bank. He moved like a short-legged, blocky bull. He had a huge ball of a head set on a muscular neck, his shoulders were wide and thick, his arms and hands were big, but oddly enough, his legs were so thin and spindling that it seemed nothing else than a miracle would give the strength they must have to carry his massive body.

Morgan wheeled to glare at Bud. 'Your father's coming across the street now. What was the idea of telling me he was in his office?'

Bud sat back in his chair and laughed. He was still laughing when Lamm came in and turned the lock on the door. He said, 'Dad, Dillard's sore at me. He came in and asked for you and I let him think you were in your office.'

Lamm chuckled. 'Bud has a great sense of humor, Dillard. Come on back. I'm here now.'

Morgan followed Kirk Lamm into his office. So Bud had a great sense of humor, did he? He must have inherited it, Morgan thought, because the banker had the same caliber of humor. He probably laughed every time he foreclosed on a ranch.

Lamm sat down at his desk, took a cigar from a box that was in front of him, and bit off the end. 'What was it you wanted, Dillard?'

'I want to borrow five hundred dollars,' Morgan said. 'I'm running out of hay and the grass won't be up for several weeks. I'd like to buy a few young steers, too. I can get them from some of the big outfits down Peace Creek and make a good profit on them by fall.'

'You're back on your interest, aren't you?' Lamm asked as if he didn't know.

'A little,' Morgan answered.

Lamm rose and walked across the room to a file cabinet. He took out a large manila envelope marked Morgan Dillard, Rafter D, and, returning to the desk, removed the contents from the envelope and scanned a

4

sheet of paper.

'Well, let's see now,' Lamm mumbled. 'Five years ago you were working for Lee Jameson out here on the Dry Fork, then four years ago you bought the Rafter D on the other side of the mountains. You took your money out of the bank and put it into the ranch. Hmmm, about eight hundred dollars, wasn't it? You borrowed the rest from the bank. Lee Jameson recommended you for the loan. He said you were a hard worker.' Lamm looked up. 'Of course you realize that Jameson's word doesn't amount to anything now.'

'Why?'

'He's broke. Everybody out there on Poverty Flat is broke. I don't know how they hang on.'

Morgan knew that what used to be called the Dry Fork valley was known now as Poverty Flat because the Smoky River Land Development Company, of which Kirk Lamm was president, had stolen water that had irrigated the Dry Fork valley for years. Morgan opened his mouth to say that Jameson wouldn't be broke if Lamm hadn't stolen the water, but he didn't say it. Anything he said along that line would destroy the slim chance he had of getting the loan.

Lamm had dropped his gaze to the paper he held in his hand and was mumbling again.

5

'You're twenty-five years old, you're unmarried, and you have title to a quarter section of meadow land along the creek. It says here you've got fifty head of cattle. All this information correct?'

It wasn't, because Morgan had lost three cows during the winter. The rest of the stock had come through in poor shape. If he didn't lose several more before summer he'd be lucky, but he wasn't going to tell Lamm that.

'That's about it,' Morgan said.

'You are back in your interest,' Lamm said. 'You were right about that.' He looked up again. 'You think you would be better off if you had more hay and more cattle and more interest to pay?'

Morgan reached for tobacco and paper, then dropped his hand. This action was strictly from habit. He hadn't had money to buy tobacco since the first of the year, but on an occasion like this when he felt the need for a cigarette, he simply didn't realize that it had been four months since he'd had a smoke.

'Yes,' Morgan said. 'I wouldn't have made the ride over here if I didn't.'

Lamm remained silent for a time, but continued to study the paper in front of him as he chewed on his cold cigar, then he laid the paper down. He said, 'I have already loaned you more than your shirttail outfit is worth, Dillard. If I loaned you another

6

nickel, I would be throwing good money after bad. I let you hold on even after you failed to pay your interest last fall, but you had better know right now that I will not be so generous this fall.'

Morgan's hands fisted and closed and fisted again. He felt a deadly cold settle into his belly and run down into his legs. His head throbbed as little red dots flashed across his vision. He whirled and stalked out of the office and across the bank to the front door. He heard Bud's jeering laugh but he didn't turn around. He turned the lock and, opening the door, stepped outside. Someday a man would walk in there and kill Kirk Lamm. If he hadn't got out, he might have been that man.

For a time Kirk stood beside his horse, thinking of the long days of hard work he had put into the Rafter D, of his plans and dreams that were going up in a cloud of smoke, of his hopes of marrying Mamie Albert who lived on the next spread. If he didn't borrow some money, he didn't have a chance and he'd lose the Rafter D come fall. He guessed he'd known all the time that he wouldn't get the loan, but they say a drowning man clutches at straws and he was surely a drowning man.

He untied his sorrel, but he didn't mount for a moment. The stage had just turned into Main Street and was wheeling hellbent toward the hotel. The driver pulled up in a rolling bank of dust and swung down. Several men including Sheriff Frank Nolan were waiting in front of the hotel to see who had come in on the stage.

Morgan waited, standing with one hand on the saddle horn as he watched the passenger stagger into the hotel. The ride up the Dry Fork was a rough one and Morgan remembered that the stage often stopped at the Jameson ranch for the passengers to stretch their legs and get a drink of water.

He dreaded the long ride back to the Rafter D, but there was nothing for him here in Harmony. When he thought about Lee Jameson and his neighbors living out there in fields of dry sand that had been green only a few years before, he decided he wasn't so bad off. He watched the stage driver climb back to the high seat, pick up the lines and drive across the street and stop in front of the bank. Kirk Lamm and Bud came out and took the strong box, Lamm asking, 'No trouble?'

'Not a bit,' the driver said, 'but I'm glad to get rid of that much dinero. I could see a road agent hiding behind every bush when I was coming up the Dry Fork.'

Irritated at the driver's remark about 'that much dinero,' Kirk Lamm shot an apprehensive glance at Morgan as if afraid he might pull his gun and take the strong box.

Quickly, Lamm and his son carried the box into the bank, almost scurrying in their haste. Morgan laughed as he swung into the saddle. They made a strange looking pair, the tall skinny boy and his short-legged, massive father.

The stage driver was staring at Morgan. He called, 'Say, you're Morgan Dillard, ain't you? Used to work for Lee Jameson?'

'That's right,' Morgan said. 'I didn't notice who you were, Buck. How's things?'

The driver shrugged. 'Cold coming up the Dry Fork. Just two seasons in this country, August and winter, and August is a long time coming.'

'How is it on the Grand?'

'Spring got there two, three weeks ago,' the driver answered. 'The weather's been wonderful. Been out on the Dry Fork lately?'

'No,' Morgan said, 'but I hear Jameson and the rest are busted.'

The driver nodded. 'Busted flat. Been busted ever since these highbinders in town stole the water. Funny thing, Dillard. If you'd held me up and stolen that strong box, you'd have been arrested and sent up for twenty years, but Lamm and Nolan and their pals can steal water and it don't seem to be no crime.' He leaned forward and spat over the wheel. 'Damn it, Dillard, I dunno. I wouldn't blame Jameson and Pony Bartlett and the rest of 'em if they rode into town and shot hell out of it.'

'I wouldn't, either,' Morgan said. 'If I lived on this side of the Catclaws, I'd help 'em. How's Laurie?'

'You ain't seen her since you quit working out there?'

'That's right. Been more'n four years.'

'She's growed up to be a mighty purty woman. She's sure the apple of Lee's eye. Well, I got to put this rig away.'

'So long, Buck,' Morgan said, and rode down the street.

He took the road that followed Smoky River into the Catclaws, his thoughts on Lee Jameson. The man was middle-aged, beaten and broke because his water had been stolen and, because the power in the county was on Kirk Lamm's side, there was nothing Jameson could do about it.

Still, Jameson hadn't given up, although he'd have to in time. He had a wife and daughter, and all three of them were starving to death. Where would they go and what would they do? It was a shame for Jameson to start working for wages at his age, but that was probably what he'd have to do.

A violent anger took possession of Morgan, a smoldering anger directed at Lamm—not so much because of his trouble, because he was young and could start over, but because of what had happened to Jameson and Pony Bartlett and the rest of the ranchers on the Dry Fork. Somewhere, somehow, he told himself, Kirk Lamm would be punished. It was only fair that he would be.

CHAPTER TWO

They rode into Harmony at high noon on the following day, Pony Bartlett in front on his black gelding, Laurie Jameson to his right and a little behind him, and Banjo Smith and Doak Watts in the rear. They reined up in front of the Harmony State Bank and dismounted, slowly and casually as if this was an ordinary business trip into town.

The chill wind slashed at them, driving down from the Catclaws on the west and stirring the dust. The winter had been a dry one and there was very little snow in the mountains. Even the Smoky River was low. Dust on the block-long Main Street was hockdeep.

Laurie didn't carry a gun, but she was wearing a man's shirt, Levi's, a sheepskin coat, and a flat-topped Stetson pulled low over her eyes. Very few people were on the street because of the cold wind and the blowing dust, and this was the way Bartlett and the others wanted it. Anyone glancing casually from a window on Main Street or

11

walking rapidly past the bank would have looked at Laurie and taken her for a teenage boy. This, too, was the way they wanted it.

Pony Bartlett walked into the bank, Banjo Smith and Doak Watts following. Laurie remained outside, holding the horses. Two customers were standing in front of the teller's cage. Bartlett stopped behind the second one, waiting until they finished their business. Banjo and Doak moved to a street window and stood looking out, their hands in their pockets.

Bud Lamm was behind the teller's window. Kirk Lamm wasn't in sight and the door to his private office in the rear of the building was open. When the second customer stepped aside, Pony Bartlett moved up to the window and said, 'How are you, Bud?'

Bud Lamm grinned at him. He probably thought that Pony was here to ask for a loan again. This time it would be Bud's pleasure to say no because his father was having dinner in the Harmony Hotel dining room with Sheriff Frank Nolan.

'I'm fine, Pony,' Bud Lamm said. 'How's things out on Poverty Flat?'

Pony didn't grin and he didn't say anything for a moment. He knew that folks in Harmony liked to call the Dry Fork country Poverty Flat. It had been exactly that for the last three years, ever since Kirk

Lamm had started the Smoky River Land Development Company and had built the dam above town. The company had cut off the water which had flowed through the Dry Fork canal for twenty years. The whole operation was illegal, but it took money to fight such a case down through the courts, and no one on the Dry Fork had any money.

Pony had all he could do to keep from pulling his gun and shooting the grin off Bud Lamm's smirking face, but he knew he could not permit himself that luxury, not yet anyway, so he said, 'We're still starving, Bud.'

Young Lamm's grin widened. 'Maybe you can get credit at the Mercantile.'

He knew better, and Pony knew that he knew it. Pony had often said that if you put all of the business men of Harmony into a sack and shook them up, they'd come out shaped like dollar signs. Orlando Craig who owned the Mercantile, Doc Vance, Frank Nolan; they were exactly the same breed of cats as Kirk Lamm, and the four of them were partners in the Smoky River Land Development Company.

'I doubt that the Mercantile would give me any credit,' Pony said.

'Then you must be here to ask for a loan from the bank,' Budd said, and laughed, making a grating sound that rubbed Pony's spine like sandpaper.

Banjo Smith said, 'All right, Pony. Looks clear.'

Banjo and Doak Watts wheeled away from the window and moved swiftly through the swinging gate between the teller's cage and the wall just as Pony drew his revolver and lined it on Bud's chest. He said, 'That's right. I'm asking for a loan.' He shoved a flour sack through the teller's window. 'Put all your paper money and gold into the sack. I don't want the silver.'

Bud's lips parted, his eyes widened, and he began to shake. 'Have you gone loco, Pony?'

'No,' Pony answered. 'It's just that your pa has always been a great hand for asking about collateral. Right now I own the best collateral in the world. It's in my right hand with five loads in the cylinder. Unless you want to find out how this collateral feels ripping through your hide, you'll start doing what I told you.'

Banjo and Doak had pulled the safe door open, Banjo calling, 'Looks like we had the right tip.'

Bud's teeth were chattering. He said, 'Don't shoot me, Pony, but I can't do what you're asking. You know Pa. You know what he'd do to me.'

'You'd better get it through your bone head what I'll do, you snivelling son of a bitch,' Pony said softly. 'I promise I'll kill you if you don't do exactly what I tell you,

14

and I'll surely kill you if you make a move for that pistol you've got under the counter.'

Bud took the flour sack, his hands trembling, and began scooping gold into it. He managed to say in a quavering voice, 'They'll hang you, Pony. You'll never get away with a stupid trick like this.'

'I think we will,' Pony said.

Bud shoved the partly filled sack through the window. 'That's all there is.'

Pony suspected he was lying, but it wasn't worth going around the counter to look for himself. Banjo and Doak ran through the gate, each carrying a partly filled flour sack. Banjo said, 'I never seen so much dinero, Pony. Must be fifty thousand here, just like we heard.'

Pony said, 'Get on your horses,' and backed toward the door.

Banjo and Doak ran out ahead of him. Bud gripped the edge of the marble counter, his face deathly white, his teeth still chattering. Just as Pony reached the door, Bud grabbed the revolver that Kirk Lamm had left here for exactly this purpose. Bud had almost leveled the barrel when Pony fired, the bullet hitting the boy in the chest and knocking him down.

Pony wheeled and ran, holstering his gun before he reached his horse. The other three were already in their saddles. Pony took the reins from Laurie and headed west on the

15

road that led to the Dry Fork country. The others followed close behind.

The shot stirred the town and brought men running into the street, but there was so much dust in the air that no one could see clearly enough to be sure what had happened. Pony held the hard pace for half a mile, then slowed up. No one had as much as fired a shot at them. Pony grinned at Laurie. 'Smooth as silk,' he said.

'You promised there wouldn't be any shooting,' Laurie said accusingly. 'Now they'll hang us if they catch us.'

'Then we'd better make sure they don't catch us,' Pony said.

'You kill him?' Banjo asked.

'He'll die if he ain't dead already,' Pony answered with satisfaction. 'I wish it had been his old man. Or Doc Vance.'

No one said anything for another mile. Laurie knew what was in Pony's mind. It took a lot of hell to push ordinary, lawabiding people into robbing a bank; it took a lot more to push them into murder. She was sure that Pony didn't have the slightest regret over killing Bud Lamm, unless the regret was that he had not killed Bud's father or the doctor.

She shivered as a blast of cold air swept across the sagebrush flat. She pulled the collar of her coat closer around her neck, wondering if anyone in Harmony had

16

recognized her. Probably not, with the wind blowing and all that dust in the air. Not many people in Harmony knew her any more.

There just hadn't been any reason to go to town lately. Not when you don't have money and folks look at you as if you were some kind of crawling thing just because you're dirt poor. Maybe it was crazy pride that made you think you looked that way. She didn't know, but she did know from hard experience that she hadn't been welcome in the Mercantile any more than Pony Bartlett was welcome in the bank.

Of all the people who had somehow managed to exist out here on the Dry Fork, Pony Bartlett had the greatest reason to hate the Harmony people, most of all Kirk Lamm and Doc Vance. There had been a time when water had flowed through the canal and Bartlett had owned one of the finest ranches in Dry Fork valley, but when the water had been diverted, he had lost everything, including his wife and baby.

Laurie remembered what had happened with a poignant grief that was almost agony. She had been very fond of Mrs Bartlett and the baby. They had come down with a high fever last November and Bartlett had ridden to Harmony through a hard snowstorm to get Doc Vance, but he had trouble locating him. When he did run the doctor down,

17

he found him playing poker in a hotel room with the sheriff and Kirk Lamm and Orlando Craig. He wouldn't leave until Bartlett pulled a gun and made him go.

They had lost more time in one way or another in spite of Bartlett's threats. When they reached Pony's ranch, Mrs Bartlett and the baby were dead. Malnutrition, Vance had said, and it was probably the truth because the Bartletts, like everyone else on the Dry Fork, had been close to starving for months. It had always seemed to Laurie that Kirk Lamm had been responsible for the death of Mrs Bartlett and the baby, that he should have been tried for murder, but of course he wouldn't be, not in this county.

In the last six months Laurie had seen Pony Bartlett change from a happy, smiling man to a somber one who looked old at the age of thirty, his face as deeply lined as her father's who was nearly twice Bartlett's age. She understood this and sympathized with him, and when the idea of robbing Kirk Lamm's bank had occurred to her, she had gone to Bartlett with it. He had picked up the idea at once, he had worked out the details, and had enlisted Banjo Smith and Doak Watts.

Pony had tried to talk Laurie into staying at home, but she had refused. Besides, they needed someone to hold the horses, and Pony had admitted that the job would take

18

three men inside the bank on the chance that both Kirk Lamm and Bud would be there, or that someone else might be in the bank and it would take another gun to keep them from making trouble.

Still, the possibility of murder had not occurred to her, and Laurie knew, with conditions being what they were in Harmony, that Bud Lamm's death would be called murder no matter what he had done to provoke it.

They made a wide swing when they reached a stretch of hardpan east of town. Reversing themselves, they headed for the Catclaws. They reached Smoky River in the middle of the afternoon, a slow-moving, meandering stream at this point with willows lining the banks.

They watered the horses and took a short rest. Laurie, looking at the muddy river, thought she had never seen it so low. The dam was two miles below here, and although the water was normally backed up past where they were, there was no sign of the dam-made lake today.

Laurie sucked in a long breath and glanced at Pony Bartlett's wooden face. Her folks had called her a tomboy and she guessed she was. She was an only child, and had become a tomboy from necessity more than choice because she'd worked with her father the same as a boy would at everything from haying to branding.

Now she had helped rob a bank. She was eighteen, but she had never been in love unless she counted the puppy love she'd had for Morgan Dillard who had worked for her folks the year she was thirteen. He had a ranch in the other side of the Catclaws, or so she had heard, but she hadn't seen him for more than four years. He probably wouldn't remember her.

Actually Laurie had never really had a beau, although Banjo Smith had taken her to a box supper and a spelling match and a few of the other gatherings at the Dry Fork schoolhouse. Sometimes she wondered if Banjo or Doak or even Pony Bartlett ever thought of her as a woman.

Suddenly the enormity of what they had done hit her as it had not hit her before. She'd go to prison. Instead of helping her folks as she had planned, she'd disgraced them just as Banjo and Doak had disgraced their parents. Maybe they'd even hang her.

She took another long breath and burst out, 'Pony, you promised there wouldn't be any killing.'

'He pulled a gun on me after I warned him not to,' Bartlett said. 'What did you want me to do, let him shoot me down and then run to the door and shoot all three of you?'

'But they'll call it murder,' she cried. 'It isn't just bank robbery now.'

20

'That's right,' Bartlett agreed. 'If the sheriff catches us, he won't bother with taking us to jail. You'll be shot down the same as if you was a man. You should have thought of that a little sooner.' He stepped into the saddle. 'Let's ride.'

She mounted and followed him, knowing there was nothing she could say or do. It was too late. She had accepted a man's role and she had better be prepared to follow it through to the bitter end.

They rode up the river, entering the canyon and climbing steadily into the Catclaws as granite walls closed in on them and rose higher and higher on both sides. She knew as well as if she had been told that there was only one solution. They must never let Sheriff Frank Nolan catch them.

CHAPTER THREE

Sheriff Frank Nolan and Kirk Lamm were finishing their dinner in the hotel dining room and Doc Vance had just joined them when they heard a gunshot. Nolan started to get up and then sat down when Lamm motioned at him and said, 'Just some drunk cowboy letting off steam. A couple of Hap Mulligan's boys are in town. The last I saw of them they were getting loaded in the Belle

21

Union.'

'That's right.' Doc Vance's thin lips made a quick grin, then it faded, and he added, 'Nobody would dare do anything real bad in your town, Frank.'

'It ain't my town,' Nolan said sharply. 'I ain't paid to be town marshal.'

'But you'll go on serving without pay,' Lamm said. 'With taxes being what they are, and with you getting the fat salary from the county that you do, you can't expect to have the town pay you, too.'

Nolan suddenly lost his appetite and shoved his plate back. This was the kind of talk he heard from Kirk Lamm all the time, and he'd had enough of it. 'Kirk, if there is any man in this county who has a good thing going, it's you. When you talk about a fat salary...'

'Now, now, Sheriff,' Vance said, the quick grin coming and leaving his mouth again. 'You've had your bread buttered real good, too. You might say it's the extra-curricular activities that make up the big salary. It strikes me that you got no complaint.'

Kirk Lamm nodded smugly as he took his last bite of pie. 'Correct, Doctor. If you have any complaint, Frank, hand in your star and sign over your part of the Smoky River Land Development Company to your partners.'

Nolan bowed his head and stared at his hands which were fisted on his lap. He was

22

too angry to risk saying a word. Kirk Lamm was a dictator who was able to impose his will on everyone in Harmony by one means or another. The county, too.

Lamm's latest maneuver in starting the Smoky River Land Development Company and cutting off the water that was used to irrigate the Dry Fork country was as frank a piece of thievery as Frank Nolan had ever seen. The worst part of the whole business was that Nolan was a partner in the thievery. Not that he minded it. He'd make a profit in time, and he didn't care what happened to Pony Bartlett and the Jamesons and the two or three other families that somehow existed out there on the dust pile known as Poverty Flat. What he did mind was the arbitrary way Kirk Lamm called the turn.

If you were a threat to Lamm, he simply ground you up the way you'd put a chunk of pork into a meat grinder and make sausage out of it. Nolan had just about had enough. He was very close to saying that Lamm could have the star and his share of the Smoky River Land Development Company to boot when Abner Day ran into the dining room.

'Sheriff.' Day stopped and struggled for breath, then added, 'Doc.'

Day clerked for Orlando Craig in the Mercantile, a mild and inoffensive man who would never under ordinary circumstances have interrupted Frank Nolan and Doc

23

Vance at dinner, especially when Kirk Lamm was with them.

'Well?' Nolan asked. 'What is it?'

Day took another breath and blurted, 'Bud's been shot and the bank's been robbed.'

The three men at the table simply sat there and stared stupidly at Day for several seconds. Vance was the first to shake off the paralysis that the news caused. He jumped up from the table, grabbed his derby from the hat rack near the door, picked up his black bag and ran into the street.

Nolan was the next to move. He was a tall man who simply outran the shorter legged doctor and was the first to shoulder through the crowd that had gathered around the door of the bank. He lunged through the gate at the end of the counter, then stopped and stared at Bud Lamm who lay on his back behind the teller's window, a revolver on the floor a few inches from his right hand.

Nolan saw that there was still some money under the shelf behind the teller's window, but he knew, of course, that the great bulk of the cash shipment that had come in on yesterday's stage would have been in the safe. As the doctor knelt beside Bud Lamm, Nolan turned to the safe and saw that it had been cleaned out.

Kirk Lamm had sent for the money to buy land below the Smoky River dam. The company had an option on ten thousand acres which was undeveloped rangeland, and most of the cowmen who owned it had insisted on being paid in cash.

The sheriff swung around just as Kirk Lamm came in, white-faced, his jaw set in the determined manner that was characteristic of him when his plans went wrong. He stood a few feet from Bud, waiting until Vance rose. There was a comical side to this, Nolan thought, remembering the conversation in the hotel dining room. The idea had probably never occurred to Kirk Lamm that anyone would dare enter his town and shoot his son and rob his bank and interfere with his plans. It was, Nolan told himself, nothing less than sacrilege.

Vance rose and faced Lamm. 'Dead,' he said. 'I doubt that he lived a minute after the bullet struck him.'

Lamm clenched his big fists and slowly turned to face Nolan. 'You're going to catch them, and by God, we'll hang every one of them.' Nolan had never thought Kirk Lamm had enough feelings about anything to make him cry, but tears were running down his face. 'You understand me, Frank? You're going to catch them if you have to stay in the saddle for a week.'

Nolan nodded, not wanting to talk to Lamm at the moment. The man was

25

unreasonable much of the time when he was opposed, and right now he would be more than unreasonable. Nolan walked past Lamm to the door and looked at the crowd that still clustered in front of the bank. In the back of his mind was the thought that if he had run into the street when he'd first heard the shot instead of staying at the table because Lamm told him to, he might have seen who left the bank. He might even have got off a shot or two.

'Any of you men know anything about this?' Nolan asked. 'Who they were and how many and what direction they took?'

'I was tending bar in the Belle Union,' Clint Jones said. 'I looked out of the window and I seen these four horses in the street. A lot of dust was blowing. The wind's died down now, but it was whooping it up just then so I couldn't see real good. I think a kid was holding the horses. I did see two men run out of the bank with what looked like flour sacks in their hands, then I heard a shot and another one came out. They jumped on their horses and lit a shuck out of town.'

'Why didn't you shoot?' Nolan demanded.

'I aimed to,' Jones said. 'I grabbed my greener and ran into the street, but just then the dust got worse and some of it was in my eyes. I couldn't see a damned thing, Sheriff.'

'Anybody else in the Belle Union?' Nolan asked.

Jones motioned toward the two cowboys who stood behind him, both of them plainly too drunk to be of any value as witnesses. One of them said with great gravity, 'I seen eight men run out of the bank, Sheriff. I'd have stopped 'em right there in the street, but there was too many.'

The other man nodded. He said with a straight face, 'I counted ten, Sheriff.'

Several other men had run into the street when they heard the shot, but they were all like Jones. There was too much dust just at that moment to see clearly what had happened. They might be lying about the dust, Nolan thought. Few had any money deposited in the bank. Actually most of them were in debt and probably hated Kirk Lamm, so it was more than possible that the townsmen actually sympathized with the outlaws.

The store owner, Orlando Craig, was in the crowd. He didn't say anything until he saw that Nolan was learning nothing of value, then he said, 'Frank, Abner here was in the bank just before the shot was fired.'

'Well?' Nolan demanded.

Abner Day had worked in the Mercantile as long as Frank Nolan had been in Harmony. He never drank, and Nolan judged him to be a truthful man, but now for some reason he was hesitant about saying anything. Finally Craig, impatient, gave him

27

a nudge, 'Speak up, Abner. You're the only one who saw anything.'

'That's the trouble, Sheriff,' Day said. 'I didn't see what happened. It's true I was in the bank before it happened. I was standing behind Claude Peters who was cashing a check. He wanted a certain amount of change and it seemed like it took Bud a while to count it out.'

Peters was one of the ranchers below the dam who was selling his land to the company, so Nolan discounted any idea that he was involved. Day hesitated again, and once more Craig gave him a nudge. 'Damn it, Abner, speak up.'

'I hate to get anybody into trouble,' Day said, plainly unhappy about the whole situation. 'I tell you I didn't see it happen. I was standing there behind Claude waiting my turn when Pony Bartlett came in. A couple of boys from Poverty Flat was with him. I don't know them folks like I used to 'cause they ain't been in the store much lately, but I know I've seen them boys three, four years ago. They'd growed up, so I ain't real sure of their names.'

He should have guessed, Nolan told himself. Of course it was some of the Poverty Flat bunch that had water stolen from them and now they had stolen money from the bank that had been responsible for the water being lost. In a way it was fair enough, but

28

that was a thought Frank Nolan could not afford.

'Anybody else?' Nolan asked.

Claude Peters had left town, someone said. None of the others had anything to offer except Clint Jones who added that the four men had ridden east toward Poverty Flat. Nolan ordered the livery stable owner to saddle his horse and five more including Kirk Lamm's. He picked four men to round out the posse, then he wheeled and walked into the bank to where Lamm was standing beside Bud's body.

'It was some of the Poverty Flat bunch,' Nolan said. 'Six of us will be enough to handle them. You're going along.'

Lamm shook his head. 'I've got to stay here and take care of things. Doc will have to look after the body...'

'Doc can do it without your help,' Nolan said. 'You've given orders around here for a long time. Now I'm giving them. You're going, Kirk. It won't hurt for you to get a few saddle sores on your butt. It was your kid who was shot and your bank that was robbed and you're going with the posse.'

Lamm was still in a state of shock, but now he began to come out of it. He shook his head again, his face turning stubborn. 'Not me,' he said. 'They'll head up into the Catclaws and hide out. They won't be crazy enough to ride back to their homes. It may

29

take you a week to find them, but you can do it. I can't be out of town that long.'

'You're riding into the mountains with us,' Nolan said. 'I can tell you right now that the posse won't move an inch out of town until you make up your mind to go. All you've got to do is lock up the bank. You're out of business till we get that dinero back anyhow.'

'Why are you trying to make me go?' Lamm demanded. 'You're the sheriff. It's your business, not mine.'

'It's your business because you're a member of the posse,' Nolan said. 'If you want to know why, I can soon tell you. If we don't find this bunch and recover the dinero, you'll blame us, me in particular. If you're along, we'll have your great wisdom riding with us.'

'All right, I'll go,' Lamm said reluctantly. 'Just remember that you are using my wisdom.'

'I won't forget,' Nolan said as he turned and walked out of the bank.

The crowd had disappeared, but Orlando Craig was waiting for Nolan. When the sheriff reached him, he said, 'They'll go up the Smoky River and on over the pass to Peaceful Valley, won't they?'

'I don't know,' Nolan said. 'They didn't head that way. Maybe that was just to throw us off, but if they do go over the pass and get into that lava country on the other side of Peace Creek, nobody can track 'em.'

'I thought I'd telephone Morgan Dillard before we start,' Craig said. 'If I can't get him, I'll try Steve Albert. They both live at the foot of the pass, and if this outfit beats us over there, one of 'em might spot 'em.'

Nolan hesitated, wondering if either Dillard or Albert would be as sympathetic to the posse as he would be to the outlaws. Both owed money to the bank and Lamm had been as hard on them as he was on anyone who was in debt to the bank.

Dillard had been in town yesterday afternoon. If he'd asked for a loan, he had probably been turned down. Then Nolan shrugged his shoulders, thinking it wouldn't hurt anything for Craig to call them.

'All right, go ahead,' Nolan said. 'I'll get the horses.' A sudden idea flashed through his mind and before he thought, he added, 'Tell 'em that there's a five thousand dollar reward for information leading to the capture of the outlaws and the recovery of the stolen money.'

Surprised, Craig asked, 'Who's going to put that reward up? The county?'

'No, the bank,' Nolan answered.

Craig smiled. 'Does Kirk know?'

Nolan shook his head. 'I just thought of it.'

'He won't like it,' Craig said. 'Oh, there's

31

one more thing. I pried something out of Abner that might be important. He didn't tell you because he wasn't sure, but he knows the Poverty Flat people better'n anybody else in town 'cause he's waited on 'em for years. He thinks it wasn't a boy who held the horses like Clint Jones says. He's pretty sure it was Laurie Jameson.'

'The hell!' Nolan thought about it, considering what it might mean, and decided that it would give him the leverage on Lee Jameson that he needed. 'Go ahead and make your telephone calls. We've got to get started.'

He strode rapidly toward the livery stable, knowing that the first thing he had to do was to find out if the outlaws kept on in the direction they had started or if they had turned back toward the Catclaws as Orlando Craig thought. If Lee Jameson knew, he'd get it out of him.

CHAPTER FOUR

Morgan Dillard had spent the morning riding along Peace Creek looking for grass. He did this every spring because the problem was the same every spring. The new grass was always slow starting on this side of the Catclaws, slower even than on the Smoky

River side because the altitude was a good deal higher.

He reined up on a bench above the valley and looked down at his Rafter D buildings and the hay meadows that still showed very little green. His gaze traveled on up the valley, but he saw no more green in the pasture than he did in the meadows. There was going to be a bad week or so between the day his hay gave out and the time the pasture could support his cattle. He wondered glumly how much longer he could hold on, or if there was any sense in trying. He was just about where he had been when he'd bought the outfit except that now he was behind in his interest.

His gaze drifted southward along the creek to Steve Albert's Pothook. Steve was his closest neighbor. Morgan was engaged to Steve's daughter Mamie who taught school about forty miles down the valley. He hadn't seen her since Christmas. She seldom came home between Christmas and the end of the term because of the weather, but she should be home any time now. School was usually out about the end of April.

The Rafter D and Pothook were very much alike. The creek dropped rapidly below the Albert place and the valley widened. From there on down to where the stream emptied into the Grand, the ranches were big and prosperous. Any cowman below Pothook could go to Kirk Lamm in Harmony and borrow any reasonable amount of money because of one magic word. Collateral!

The only real difference between Steve Albert's position and Morgan's was that Mamie turned her salary over to her folks and Steve used it to pay his interest. The grass and hay situation was similar. Steve fought through the same tough winters and lost as much stock as Morgan did.

Every spring Steve faced the same question Morgan did. Would he fight through another year, hoping beef prices would go up and he'd get through the winter in better shape and be able to pay something on his mortgage? Or would it be smarter to go off and leave the ranch and let Kirk Lamm see what he could do with it? After Lamm had turned him down yesterday, Morgan had almost decided that was the best thing to do.

He turned his sorrel down the trail to the creek. He'd worked like hell for the last four years, and the hard, brutal fact was that he actually had been working for Kirk Lamm. When he reached the corral, he offsaddled and put his horse away, the perennial question still unanswered.

The Rafter D had been a marginal operation from the beginning. He'd known that when he'd bought the outfit, but he'd had the enthusiasm of youth, and had counted on hard work and good luck to pull him through. Well, he'd worked hard, but good luck had been elusive.

As he walked toward his cabin, the sense of failure so completely engulfed him that he was tempted to gather up the few things he wanted to keep, saddle his sorrel and ride off. Not that the temptation was anything new. It was just stronger today because the small hope he'd had of getting a loan from the bank was gone. But he was engaged to Mamie. He simply wasn't free to ride off.

He built a fire and put the tea kettle on the front of the stove, then looked around. A poor place to live, he told himself, within these bare log walls with a table and two benches, a pine bureau that teetered precariously every time he touched it, and a bunk covered with a straw tick and a couple of ragged blankets. No place to bring a wife. In a way he hated to see Mamie when she got back because he knew she was going to say they had been engaged long enough.

Well, they had, he told himself as he picked up the water bucket and turned to the door, but that did not change the hard facts. He stopped and set the bucket down, for Steve Albert had just ridden up and dismounted.

'How are you, Morg?' Steve asked.

'If you really want to know how I am,'

35

Morgan said, 'I'll tell you. I'm damn poor.'

'Lamm turn you down yesterday?'

'That's right. This morning I've been out looking for grass, but I didn't find any.'

'Same here,' Steve said. 'Well, I came over to tell you not to fix no dinner. Mamie's home and you're supposed to eat with us. Ma killed a hen this morning. I reckon she'll be good and tender by the time you get to our place.'

Morgan leaned his long body against the door casing and scratched his week-old stubble. He was tempted to say no. He didn't feel like being neighborly and he didn't think he could stand Mrs Albert's too-cheerful conversation. Most of all, he wasn't up to arguing with Mamie about getting married.

He looked at Steve and knew he'd have to accept the invitation. He couldn't bear to see the eagerness go out of Steve's round, little face. He was forty-nine years old, but in many ways he was still a child with a child's eagerness for life and filled with a child's constant hope.

It just never occurred to Steve that if Mamie didn't give him her wages, he'd lose Pothook. Or if it did occur to him, he never permitted the thought to linger. He was always certain that the next year would be better and he would make a lot of money and pay his debt to Mamie.

'I'll be over as soon as I shave,' Morgan said. 'I couldn't face Mamie with all this brush on my face.'

'Sure, go ahead,' Steve said. 'You know, we're going to have a warm spring. The grass will pop up overnight. The robins are back and chirping. Seems like they've got ways of knowing about things like that.'

Morgan turned to the stove and felt of the tea kettle to see if the water was warm. He didn't feel like listening to Steve's optimism any more than he felt like listening to Mrs Albert's conversation. Both were like bubbling springs that just kept flowing.

The water wasn't hot yet, but it was warm. Morgan carried his razor and mug to the mirror that hung on the wall near the door. He stropped his razor, wishing Steve would go home, but Steve wasn't showing any sign of leaving. He pulled a bench away from the table and sat down, cuffing his Stetson to the back of his bald head.

'I've got news,' Steve said. 'Orlando Craig called from Harmony. He told me he tried to get you, but you didn't answer.'

Morgan brought the tea kettle from the stove and poured water into the wash basin, then carried the kettle back to the stove. 'What did he want?'

'You'd never guess,' Steve answered. 'The bank was held up at noon and they got away with more'n fifty thousand. Craig thought it

37

was about that. They figure the robbers will head over the Catclaws and go right past your place. That's why Craig tried to call you.'

Morgan lathered his face as he thought about it. Craig might be right. If the outlaws knew the country, they would probably head for the lava beds where there were caves and water, and maybe some grass in the little meadows that were islands in the lava flow. It was the best and cheapest hideout in the world, and if they had food, they could hold off a posse for weeks. Or they could ride up Peace Creek to Bardo, the old deserted mining camp.

'Well, I don't pretend to be no hero,' Steve said, 'but maybe with your help, we could nab them outlaws. Craig claimed there was a five thousand dollar reward for information that would lead to their capture and the return of the stolen money.'

Morgan had started to shave. He turned, his hand holding the razor poised at the side of his face. 'Now you're getting to the interesting part. I'll keep my eyes open.'

He shaved for a time, Steve watching him with wide, eager eyes. Finally he said, 'Craig told me something else that will interest you. The robbers came from the Dry Fork country.'

Morgan wheeled to face Steve. 'I ain't surprised. They've been pushed hard enough. Did he say who they were?'

'The only one they knew for sure was Pony Bartlett. You know him?'

'Yeah, I know him,' Morgan said. 'A hell of a fine gent. Had a wife when I was over there. A real purty girl. After I left, I heard they had a baby, then last fall he lost both of 'em.'

The eagerness left Steve's face. 'Well now, I dunno. They've been pushed some and that's a fact. Just goes to prove that if you drive a good man far enough, he'll go wrong. Seems they shot and killed Bud Lamm.' He rose. 'Guess I'd better get back and tell the women you'll be along.'

'Sure,' Morgan said. 'Just as soon as I shave.'

When he finished, he put on a clean shirt and walked down the creek. He moved slowly, enjoying the sunshine and wanting time to think about what Steve had said. Kirk Lamm was a thief any way you looked at him, and he deserved anything he got.

Still, robbing a bank was worse than stealing water because it hurt everyone in the community if the bank went broke. Killing Lamm's boy made it worse. By the time he reached the Albert place, he had made up his mind that if he had a chance to capture Pony Bartlett and his partners, he'd do it.

Mamie ran out of the house when she saw Morgan and threw her arms around him. He kissed her and held her hard, then pushed her back and looked at her. She cried a little and told him he was a scoundrel, that he hadn't written to her for more than a month. He admitted he was a scoundrel and wanted to tell her she had put on ten pounds since Christmas, but he didn't have the courage. It worried him, though, for Mamie was overfond of eating and in another twenty years she'd look like her mother who threatened the seams of every dress she wore.

'Come in,' Mamie said. 'Dinner's ready. You were awful slow getting here.'

'I had to shave,' he said. 'You wouldn't have kissed me if I hadn't.'

'I guess I would,' she said, 'even if your old whiskers stuck me. Come on.'

She took his hand and led him into the house. Mrs Albert called a greeting and told him to come to the table, that they were ready to eat. Both the Albert women were excellent cooks, and he knew they were hard workers. Mamie would make him a good wife and bear his children and love him, and he often told himself that a man could ask for nothing more.

Still, he had had his doubts about marrying Mamie, doubts that had to do mostly with his end of the bargain because he knew from what she had said at Christmas and what she had written to him afterwards that she couldn't or wouldn't be put off much longer.

When the meal was over, Mrs Albert rose ponderously from her chair and said archly, 'You young folks must have a lot to talk over. I'll take care of the dishes. You run along.'

Mamie was embarrassed, but she got up and left the house. Morgan thanked Mrs Albert for the dinner, then caught up with Mamie who was walking slowly toward the creek. She had talked very little during the meal. Now she looked directly at Morgan, her face very grave as she said, 'I'm twenty-six years old. I want my own home. I want to be a wife and I want babies. I can't go on waiting forever, even for a man I love.'

'I can't take you to the Rafter D,' he said, 'and have you starve. I'm not getting anywhere, Mamie. Four years, and I'm no better off than I was when I started.'

Her head was still tipped up to look at him. She caught her breath, then she said, 'There's one way, Morgan. Give the Rafter D up. Come and live with us. We've got enough space. We'd sleep in my room. We'd have privacy.'

'It wouldn't work,' he said. 'You know that. Two families can't live in one house. Your pa would be in the same fix I'm in if you weren't teaching and giving him everything you make.'

'I've never had a ring,' she said in a tight

41

voice, 'but if I had, I'd give it back to you. I'm breaking our engagement. There are other men in the world, you know.'

She whirled and ran into the house. He walked slowly to his cabin, not sure whether he felt worse or better. In one way he felt better. He was free now, free to hand the Rafter D back to Kirk Lamm and get on his horse and ride to the end of the earth if he wanted. And Mamie was free, too, free to find another man to marry.

Then, suddenly, he remembered what Steve Albert had told him about the bank being robbed and the reward money. He'd stay, he decided. A slim chance, maybe, but the reward was worth taking a chance on. A man could do a lot with $5,000.

CHAPTER FIVE

In spite of everything that Frank Nolan could do, he didn't get the posse out of town until mid-afternoon. He rode in the lead, Kirk Lamm beside him, and Orlando Craig and Clint Jones behind them. The blacksmith, Simon Pratt, and another man who did odd jobs around town named Zach Grant rode some distance in the rear to avoid the dust.

Kirk Lamm thought it was stupid to ride

toward Poverty Flat and he said so in no uncertain terms, contending that the logical move for the outlaws to make was to go up Smoky River and on over the Catclaws into Peaceful Valley. He said the longer the posse waited to take the same route, the longer lead the outlaws would have.

Nolan let him talk, but he kept riding east. Finally Lamm couldn't stand it any longer. 'What's the matter with you, Frank?' the banker demanded. 'I thought you were taking me along for my superior wisdom?'

'Sure, that's why we took you,' Nolan agreed, 'but I didn't promise we'd use it.'

They reached the stretch of hardpan where Nolan suspected the outlaws had left the road, but he didn't say that to Lamm. He reined to a stop and waited for Pratt and Grant to catch up. Grant knew the country better than anyone else, and Nolan always took him if he was in town when a posse was being organized. He hunted deer and elk and sold the meat in Harmony, and he knew every canyon and peak of the Catclaws so well that he could draw a detailed map of the mountains from memory. Also, he was an expert tracker. That was the principal reason Nolan liked to have him along.

'What's your guess, Zach?' Nolan asked. 'You figure they doubled back here?'

'Prob'ly.' Grant stared owlishly across the flat, then tipped his head back to look at the

43

craggy spines of the mountains that raked the sky like the protruding claws of a giant cat. 'If I was them, Sheriff, I'd go on over the pass and head up Peace Creek to Bardo. Mike Twill would hide 'em and feed 'em, and you'd have one hell of time finding 'em if you tried.'

'No chance of tracking 'em across that hardpan, is there?' Nolan asked.

'Not any,' Grant said. 'Wouldn't be nothing in the road, neither, with this wind blowing, but once we get to Smoky River and start up the canyon, I can maybe tell you something.'

Nolan nodded and hipped around in the saddle. He could see the Jameson place from here. Pony Bartlett's house was about the same distance away but to the left. On beyond were a number of places, nearly all of them deserted.

Three years ago Dry Fork valley had been green, the ranches prosperous, with water flowing in the canal, which at this point ran along the side of the road. Now the valley was a desert without a trace of green. The canal was an empty ditch, the sides caved in every few feet. If water was ever available again, the canal would take hours of work and hundreds of dollars before it could be restored to use. Nolan glanced at Lamm wondering if these thoughts ever entered the banker's mind.

Three years ago twenty-six families made a good living on the Dry Fork. They paid taxes and brought money into Harmony and added to the prosperity of the county. Only five families lived out here the last Nolan had heard and he wondered what they lived on. He shrugged his broad shoulders. Chances were the five would be gone by fall.

'Well, time's wasting,' Lamm said irritably. 'You claim you're running this posse. Why aren't we riding?'

'A man has to have time to think things out, Kirk,' Nolan said blandly. 'I guess I've thought long enough. Zach, you and Simon take a ride up to Pony Bartlett's place. Go into the house and look around. The barn and corral, too. The rest of us will visit Lee Jameson.'

Lamm exploded into a furious volley of oaths, then he shouted, 'You're a fool, Nolan. Every minute you give those killers puts them farther away, and here you are piddling around in the desert. You know as well as I do that they didn't come this way. They'd have to ride a hundred miles into Utah to find a place to hole up if they kept going in this direction.'

Nolan touched up his horse and rode on to the Jameson place, turning his head to wink at Orlando Craig and Clint Jones who were behind him. They were both uneasy, for no one, not even Sheriff Frank Nolan, had ever overlooked Kirk Lamm this way.

'I'm going back to town,' Lamm said when he saw that Nolan was ignoring him. 'I refuse to have anything to do with a fool like you. I'm wondering if you aren't letting them get away on purpose.'

'You go back to town,' Nolan said, 'and the posse goes with you. For once in my life I'm giving you orders and it's a real pleasure. I've looked forward to this for years.'

'So that's it,' Lamm fumed. 'I suppose it doesn't make any difference to you that it was my boy who got killed. You don't have any children around here who could ... could...' Lamm stopped, suddenly aware of the flinty expression that had come into Nolan's gray eyes.

There was very little that had been good in Frank Nolan's life, not in the last ten years since his wife had left him with a boy and girl to raise. He had raised them, but by his stern and unyielding standards. After they were grown the girl had run off with a drummer and the boy had ridden away without even saying good-bye. The last anyone in Harmony had heard of him, he was riding for an outfit near Durango.

Even worse for Frank Nolan's peace of mind was the constant yielding to Kirk Lamm's orders. Nolan had found himself fighting a growing urge to drive his fist into Lamm's doughy belly. He had always

46

controlled this urge, but now the satisfaction of bending Lamm to his will was honey sweet. A few hours ago the man had everything, but the chances were good that he would have nothing when this was over, not even his life.

They reined up in the Jameson yard. There was no garden, no flowers, no lawn, and even the poplars that lined the front of the house were tall, gray ghosts, their brittle limbs clacking in the wind. Again Nolan glanced at Lamm, wondering if he had any notion about what the Smoky River Land Development Company had done to these people. Not that Nolan had any sympathy for them. A man who insisted on playing a losing hand was a fool.

Apparently Jameson heard the horses, for he stepped out of the barn, holding a bridle he had been repairing. He was a tall, thin man who looked almost as ghostly as the dead poplars in front of the house. He was plainly frightened when he saw who his visitors were; he stood poised as if ready for flight, his gaze darting from one man to another and coming back to rest on Nolan who dismounted and walked slowly toward him.

Nolan didn't say a word until he was within two steps of Jameson, then he asked, 'Who lives out here on the Dry Fork besides you and Pony Bartlett?'

47

'The Smiths, the Watts family, and the Winslows,' Jameson answered, 'but the Winslows are leaving. They might be gone now.'

'Any of these families have sons?' Nolan asked. 'Young, maybe twenty?'

'You know all of us, Sheriff,' Jameson said nervously. 'Why're you asking me things like that.'

'I forget,' Nolan said. 'I don't see much of you folks any more.'

Jameson swallowed, glancing at Lamm, then he brought his gaze back to Nolan's face. 'No reason for us to come to town. The bank won't loan us money and Craig won't give us credit. Not since you stole our water.'

'Stole is an ugly word, Jameson,' Nolan said, his voice deceptively soft. 'Now about these boys?'

'There's Banjo Smith,' Jameson said. 'The Watts family have a boy named Doak. He just got home from cowboying in the San Luis valley. Banjo's been here all winter. That's all. Just the two of 'em.'

'You see 'em today?'

'Yeah, both boys rode in about ten o'clock this morning. Why?'

'Where's your daughter?'

'I dunno. She rode off with the boys. They probably went to see Pony Bartlett. Laurie goes over there once a week to clean up his house. That's just since his wife died.'

'What did they do after they got to Bartlett's place?'

'How do I know? I ain't seen Laurie since.'

Nolan hit him low in the belly. Jameson bent forward, unable to get his breath, his face distorted by pain. Nolan struck him again, this time on the side of the head, knocking him to the ground where he writhed in agony.

'Look out,' Clint Jones yelled.

Nolan turned in time to see Mrs Jameson running toward him, a shotgun in her hands. As Nolan turned, she raised the gun to fire it, but Orlando Craig spurred his horse at her and she spun away from the horse to keep from being knocked down. Craig reached down and yanked the shotgun out of her hands.

'You animals,' Mrs Jameson screamed. 'You dirty, filthy animals. You steal our water and you starve us to death, and now you come out here and beat my husband to death.'

Nolan ignored her. He turned back to Jameson who was still on the ground. 'Your daughter helped hold up the bank today. Bud Lamm was shot and killed. I want to know where she went and what she did after she left here.'

Jameson had enough breath to say, 'You're a liar. Laurie wouldn't—'

Nolan kicked Jameson in the ribs, brutally

49

and needlessly. He asked again, 'Where did she go after she left here?'

'They don't know, Frank,' Orlando Craig said nervously. 'You can't beat information out of people if they don't know it.'

'Thank you, Orlando,' Nolan snarled sarcastically as he turned to his horse and mounted.

Nolan swung the animal around and touched him lightly with his spurs, his face a grim mask. Somehow he felt better. It had eased his nerves to beat and kick Lee Jameson, and when he glanced at Lamm's pale face, he felt again the wild and almost compelling urge to haul him out of the saddle and give him the same treatment he had given Jameson.

Not that there was any sense to what he had done except that he had satisfied himself that Laurie and the three men had not returned to the Dry Fork. It was just that he had lived with frustration and an inward sense of failure for so long that he was glad to have something to do, someone to beat, and, if the posse was lucky, someone to hang.

Nolan saw Pratt and Grant riding toward them and stopped to wait. When they came up, Grant said, 'No one there, Sheriff. His stock's all gone. Nothing in the kitchen or pantry to eat. Just nothing.'

Nolan nodded. He hipped around in the saddle to look at Craig. 'Orlando, you and

Clint go to town and fill up a couple of sacks with grub. We'll camp tonight in Harney Park.'

Craig nodded and started toward home, Clint Jones riding beside him. Lamm was scared and nervous, his face twitching, but still he made himself say, 'Don't you want to catch these men? Even if the Jameson girl is with them, I don't see...'

'No, you don't see,' Nolan said softly. 'Well, I didn't aim for you to see. We're having a good time, so I figure we'll just stretch it out as long as we can. No fun if we catch 'em tonight.' He paused, his eyes narrowing, then he added, 'You know, Kirk, I think I'm going to have an excuse to do something I've wanted to do for a long time.'

He touched his horse up again, noticing that Lamm didn't ask him what he wanted to do. Probably the banker knew. Nolan struck out across the hardpan toward the mountains where the Smoky River came out of the canyon. At that point there was a grassy flat called Harney Park, the best camping place anywhere on the river.

In the morning they'd go on up the canyon. Old man Higgins who had a place near the pass would know if the bandits had gone by. If they had, the next move would be to go on down to Peace Creek and talk to Morgan Dillard or Steve Albert. Grant was probably right. The four bandits would

51

almost certainly turn up the creek to Bardo where they knew they would be given a hideout.

Nolan glanced at Lamm and suddenly realized he felt good, better than he had for a long time. He didn't really care if they got the money back or if the bank failed, or even if the Smoky River Land Development Company went broke. It was worth it just to have Kirk Lamm on his knees, and that was where he was going to stay.

CHAPTER SIX

Pony Bartlett didn't stop except to blow the horses until the sun had dropped down over the top of the peaks. By the time Bartlett was ready to camp, they were almost to the summit. The north and south forks of Smoky River came together at this point, forming a small park. The road ran on up the grade and over a saddle between two peaks and followed Short Creek to Peaceful Valley. The Higgins ranch lay at the upper end of the park, hidden from Bartlett and the others by a thick growth of quakies.

Laurie knew Higgins well, or Old Hig as he was usually called, because she and her father had gone to his place every fall for the last six years to hunt. He owned a saddle horse, a pack animal, and a small band of sheep. For a small fee he would take his pack horse and bring the deer or elk that had been killed out to the road. There the meat could be loaded into wagons and hauled down the canyon.

Bartlett dismounted, tossed the sack of money to the ground, and untied another sack from behind his saddle. It contained a frying pan and two sides of bacon, the only food that he'd had in his house. All of them contributed some food, the other three stealing from their folks' kitchen. Laurie had a small sack of flour, Banjo Smith coffee and a coffee pot, and Doak Watts sugar and salt and dried prunes. He had just come home from a job and had brought most of his wages with him, so the Watts pantry was better supplied with food than the others.

Laurie stepped down, wondering what was in Pony's mind. It seemed to her that it would have been better to have ridden on over the pass. Morgan Dillard lived down there somewhere and she was sure he would help them in any way he could. But she didn't argue. Pony had been accepted as the leader and she felt she had to respect that leadership. Still, she was not prepared for what happened.

Without a word Bartlett pulled her to him and kissed her. She tasted the sweat and dust on his lips; she felt his wiry stubble scrape her face. She was so completely surprised that she did not resist him for a moment, and before she could kick or beat at him with her fists, he had released her.

'I just put my brand on her, boys,' Bartlett said, looking past her at Banjo Smith. 'I don't want no trouble with neither one of you, so don't try to vent my brand.'

Doak Watts was the younger of the two, he had not been in the valley for nearly a year, and had no particular aspirations as far as Laurie was concerned, but it was a different matter with Banjo. He had gone with Laurie, he liked her, and he probably would not have taken part in the holdup if Laurie hadn't been a member of the party.

Banjo tossed his sack of money on the ground, then stepped out of the saddle and faced Bartlett, his expression one of cold fury. 'I'm calling your bluff right now,' he said. 'Laurie's my girl. If you think...'

'No, she's mine,' Bartlett said.

Laurie stared at Banjo and then at Bartlett, still dumfounded by this quarrel which had erupted quickly and unnecessarily.

'Pony if you want to settle this—' Banjo began again.

'I've already settled it,' Bartlett cut in. 'If you don't think Laurie's my girl, why do you think she came over to my house every week and cleaned for me?'

This was too much. Laurie opened her mouth to tell Pony Bartlett what she thought of him, but he moved a foot to tap warningly against hers. She glanced at Banjo and saw him wilt under Bartlett's hard stare, saw him turn to his horse and untie the sack of grub that was behind the saddle.

'Good,' Bartlett said. 'I'll get a fire going and Laurie can start supper. You boys water the horses and stake them out above here. Don't wander off toward Old Hig's place. He can't tell the sheriff anything he don't know. I figure we'll get past his cabin before sunup in the morning.'

Doak Watts dismounted, threw his sack of money near the other two, then untied his grub sack. No one said anything until the boys left with the horses, then Laurie said, tight-lipped. 'If you think I cleaned house for you because I'm in love with you, you are the craziest man in Colorado.'

'I'm not that crazy, Laurie.' He looked at her, his faded blue eyes twinkling. 'I wish you were in love with me because you're a very pretty girl and you'd make a wonderful wife, but I don't have any illusions. I'll have to live with the memory of my wife.'

'Then will you tell me why...'

'All right, I'll tell you,' he said. 'I'm old enough to control myself, but I'm also young enough to know how a man as young as Banjo feels. You're a woman, and all three of us won't forget it even if you are wearing a man's clothes. You'll be riding with us for a long time, and there's going to be moments when temptation will be a hard thing for Banjo to buck. This way he figures he's got to whip me first.'

She didn't believe it. She thought she knew Banjo who was a decent, quiet boy. He had held her hand and had slipped an arm around her slender waist a few times, but he had never even tried to kiss her.

Pony might know what he was talking about, though. He was thirty years old, a medium-sized man with a leathery face that held a multitude of wrinkles. The last six months since his wife and baby died had put ten years on his face.

He had, Laurie knew, a streak of cruelty in him, and if he had a chance to shoot Kirk Lamm or Doc Vance or Sheriff Nolan, he would do it without a moment's hesitation. He had another side, and she had seen this part of him more than the other, a side of gentleness and compassion. As she considered this, she decided she should be grateful to him.

'All right, Pony,' she said. 'I guess I should thank you.'

He nodded, smiling a little. 'You should. Now remember we've got to act the part once in a while. I promise I won't take advantage of you.'

56

He turned away before she could say a word. She stood staring at him as he gathered wood for a fire. He was as tough as a pine knot; he could put out more work than the average man twice his size, and she had a notion that if it came to a fight between him and the two boys, he could handle both of them. Still, she was uneasy. This was something she had not considered, the fact that she was one woman with three men who were outside the law. Who knew what would happen after days and days of running?

When he returned and started the fire, she said, 'I'm scared, Pony. I didn't think I would be, but all of a sudden I am.'

'Don't be,' he said gently. 'We'll take care of you. That's one thing me'n Banjo and Doak will agree on.'

'I think we should have kept going,' she said. 'Clear on down to Peaceful Valley, maybe to Morgan Dillard's place.'

'No.'

His tone was sharp, too sharp, and she wondered what she had said that had touched his anger. She said, 'I haven't seen Morgan since he quit working for us, but I've heard you say you had. You told me you liked him. I don't see why...'

'Sure, I like him,' Bartlett said. 'I just didn't want to go down there tonight.'

'We're too close to Harmony,' she said.

57

'They could sneak up during the night.'

'One of us will stand guard so we won't be surprised,' he said. 'I don't think Nolan will make a move during the night, but if he does, we'll handle him. Now you'd better see what you can do about some supper.'

She started coffee and began slicing bacon. Maybe Pony Bartlett actually wanted the posse to try to take them. She wasn't even sure that he wanted to live After what had happened to them the last three years, it was possible that he wanted to kill Nolan and Lamm and the others more than he wanted to carry out the plan she had made and he had agreed to.

After they had eaten and Laurie had cleaned up the dishes, Bartlett said, 'Laurie's worried about the posse trying to take us tonight. If they tackle us, it'll be just before dawn, but we'll be ready for 'em if they do. Just on the slim chance that Nolan has some other idea, we'll take turns standing guard. Banjo, you'll take the first hitch, then Doak, and I'll take the last one.'

Darkness had come now, the last of the twilight blotted out by the summit to the west and the cliffs on both sides of the creek. In the shifting light from the fire, Laurie could see Bartlett's face. She didn't like what she saw. In the hours since noon he had changed. He had the look of a hunted man, and a hunted man, like any animal backed into a corner, will strike at those who had driven it into that corner.

'Pony, when I was getting supper,' Laurie said, 'I had an idea that's kind of crazy, but it might be true. I thought you acted as if you wanted them to try to take us so you'd have a chance to kill them.'

'Why not?' he asked. 'I don't want you hurt, if that's what you're thinking about, but I'll admit I want to kill them. Lamm. Nolan. Vance. Craig. They're the criminals, Laurie. They murdered my wife and baby. They stole our water. They started the whole business and I aim to see they pay for everything.'

'I want my share of the money.' Banjo nodded at the three sacks laying near the fire. 'Trying to get revenge is crazy, Pony. We've got ourselves to think about. I say split the money and separate. Each of us can go where he wants to.'

'No,' Pony said. 'We've got to stick together till we know we're in the clear. I ain't going after the posse, Laurie. Maybe that's what's been worrying you. If it is, forget it. I'm like Banjo. I want the money. I want to live, but I aim to make them pay, too. Maybe taking the money is enough. I hope it wipes Lamm out. Might be he'll shoot himself and save me the trouble.'

'We didn't plan to keep the money,' Laurie cried. 'Pony, this was my idea. You agreed to—'

'Sure,' Bartlett said tolerantly. 'You didn't really aim to turn outlaw. You were just going to use the money as a hostage and hold onto it until we negotiated with 'em to give us back our water. You're a child, Laurie. We let you think that was what we were going to do, but what you never figured out is that Lamm and his bunch won't negotiate. They'll hunt us until we kill 'em or they kill us. That's why we've got to stick together, Banjo. For a while, anyway.'

'But Pony, you said...,' Laurie wailed.

'I know what I said,' Bartlett broke in. 'Well, everything's changed. It changed the minute I killed Bud Lamm. It's too late to go to them and say we'll give you the money if you'll give our water back, so we'll keep the money and we'll run. If it comes to a fight, we'll kill them, Laurie. It's that simple. Don't forget one thing. They'll hang you or shoot you the same as they would me or Banjo or Doak. Now let's get some sleep.'

Laurie stared at Bartlett, clenching her fists. She'd been a child, had she? Well, she wasn't so much of a child that she didn't see through Pony Bartlett. He had never intended to negotiate. They had planned to keep the money from the start. All right, she'd been lied to and now she knew what she was going to do.

She took her saddle and blanket and made

her bed some distance from the fire which had died down until it was only a bed of coals. She lay down and pulled the blanket over her, staring at the ribbon of sky above her. She had a hunch that Banjo would drop off to sleep. It was black dark now, and there would be no moon for at least two hours.

Laurie had never been so angry in her life. She had trusted Pony Bartlett and he had double crossed her. Most of the anger was directed at herself for being stupid, but the fact that she had been stupid once didn't mean she had to go on being stupid.

She was tired and sleepy. Only her anger kept her awake. She heard the pound of the river, the howling of coyotes from the rims, but she kept her eyes open as she waited for Banjo Smith to drop off to sleep.

CHAPTER SEVEN

When the posse reached the river, Frank Nolan said, 'We'll camp here tonight. Orlando and Clint will be along pretty soon with the grub.'.

They dismounted, pulled gear from their horses, watered them, and staked the animals out on the flat. Lamm withdrew from the others and, walking to the bank, sat down and fired a cigar. Nolan glanced at him, amused. He was like a sulky child who, not having his own way, refused to play with his friends.

Zach Grant walked the other way to the road and got down on his hands and knees and carefully examined the tracks. Simon Pratt gathered driftwood and built a fire. Nolan paced back and forth, ignoring Lamm. He wasn't sure he was calling this right. He was reasonably certain of only one thing. The bank robbers would not go either north or south because the country along the base of the mountains was well settled and they would be seen.

There were, the way Nolan saw it, only two logical routes for them to take, across Dry Fork valley and the desert into Utah, or over the pass. He was going on the assumption that Abner Day was right and had recognized Laurie Jameson as the horse holder. That was why he felt sure that if they had gone across Poverty Flat, they would have stopped at the Jameson place and Laurie's folks would have known what she had done and where she was going.

Nolan realized that Lee Jameson might have lied, but the man didn't strike him as the kind who could stand up under a beating and go on lying. He was convinced that Orlando Craig had been right. You couldn't get information out of the people who didn't have it. Besides, the ride across the desert

62

into Utah was a hell of a tough trip for anyone, but for a girl it would be sheer torture.

Nolan turned to the fire. Grant had joined Pratt. The two men had fired their pipes and were hunkered beside the flames. Nolan said, 'Zach, let's figure on this a little. We think the horse holder was the Jameson girl. She's about half boy, ain't she?'

Grant grinned. 'Well no, she's plenty of woman, Sheriff, but she can do just about anything a man can. I've seen her and her pa and Old Hig hunt up here in the mountains, and by glory, she can ride and hike and shoot with the best of 'em.'

Nolan jerked his head toward the road. 'Find any tracks?'

Grant nodded. 'Four horses went upstream, all right. Two, three hours ago, maybe more. I reckon it's them. Ain't much traffic on this road.'

'They can't get on over the pass to Peace Creek before dark,' Nolan said thoughtfully. 'It's my guess they'll camp up there near the top. The moon won't be up till late, so it would be darker'n a bull's gut going down Short Creek.'

'I ain't augerin' with the way you're thinking,' Grant said, 'but I know Pony Bartlett purty well. He's a sullen dog right now, just waiting for a chance to bite. Now he don't know you've got Lamm in the posse, but he's gonna figure you might have him. Likewise you might have Doc Vance and Orlando Craig, so you know what he's gonna think?'

'Yeah, I can guess,' Nolan answered. 'He's going to think it'd be a prime idea to shoot a few holes in our hides.'

'That's right,' Grant agreed. 'He might even be a little more anxious to do that than to get away with the money, though I figure he'll want to do both.'

Nolan nodded. 'That's about the way I see it. With the canyon as narrow as it is, they could ambush us up there and blow our heads off before we knew they'd even seen us.'

'Well, what I'm thinking is that I ought to ride on up the canyon,' Grant said. 'They won't know I'm a member of the posse. Seeing as I know both Bartlett and the girl, I might be able to talk to 'em and find out what they're fixing to do. Pretend I was on their side, maybe. In any case, looks to me like I can find out where they are. We ought to be on our way afore sunup. If we have any luck tomorrow, I figure we can outrun 'em.'

'You'd be taking a big chance,' Nolan said. 'Suppose they figure you're one of us? They'd drill you the minute you showed your face. When they plugged Bud Lamm, they made rope bait out of themselves.'

'I know it,' Grant said. 'There's a reward

out for 'em, ain't there?'

Nolan hesitated, glancing at Lamm who was still sitting on the bank of the river, his back to them. Might as well play it all the way, Nolan decided. He said, 'Five thousand dollars.'

Grant's leathery face brightened. 'If I done something like this, I'd get me a good chunk of that dinero, wouldn't I?'

'You sure would,' Nolan answered. 'It would have to be divided, though.'

Grant nodded and, picking up a stick, poked at the fire. 'There's something else, Sheriff. I don't have no reason to like that Dry Fork bunch. You know how it's been with me. I've made part of my living killing game and selling meat. I reckon I've bent the law a mite, but you never seemed concerned about it.'

Nolan grinned, winking at Pratt. 'You've been a good man on a lot of posses, Zach.'

'That's the way it strikes me,' Grant said. 'I've helped you out when you needed me, and you always looked the other way when I was giving the law a few twists, but that bunch hires Old Hig to pack their meat out to the road and they seemed to think I'm some kind of a criminal for what I do. They've given me hell more'n once and even took a shot at me. I think Old Hig done it, but they're all the same caliber.'

'We'll find out about that,' Nolan said.

'We'll quiz Old Hig when we get to his place. If he claims he don't know nothing, we'll work him over a little.'

'Give me a chance to work on him,' Grant said. 'I hate that old bastard. Well, I'll saddle up and start out. Maybe I won't get back till morning, but don't start shooting just because you know somebody's on the trail ahead of you. Might be me.'

'We'll be careful,' Nolan said. 'You do the same. We've got lots of time. I don't think this bunch will go very far, not with three of 'em having folks still living on the Dry Fork.'

'I won't take no chances,' Grant said. 'If it don't look right, I won't go on in.'

After he left, Pratt looked at Nolan. He said, 'I ain't no smart man, Sheriff, but I know that bucko. What do you figure he's up to?'

'He'll try to fetch 'em in,' Nolan answered, 'and he'll probably get himself killed doing it. On the other hand, if he pulls it off, he can claim most of the reward.'

'If you think he'll get himself killed,' Pratt asked, 'why did you let him go?'

Nolan shrugged. 'It was his idea, not mine. I figured that he'd get one or two of them while they were shooting him. He might fetch 'em in. He's man enough to do it if he's lucky.'

Orlando Craig and Clint Jones arrived with enough food to last a week. Nolan knew they might take that much time to run their quarry down. If Bartlett and his friends hid out in the lava country beyond Morgan Dillard's ranch, the chances were a week wouldn't be enough. On the other hand, if they sought refuge with Mike Twill in Bardo, he'd have them in two days.

Nolan had an agreement with Twill that worked out well. Twill paid him to stay out of Bardo, and he did unless he was after someone who was wanted for a local crime. If that happened, Twill helped without appearing to, but any ridge runner from outside the county was safe in Bardo as long as he could pay the fare.

The sun was down by the time supper was ready. Craig called Lamm who said he wasn't hungry. Craig looked at Nolan and shook his head.

'This ain't right, Frank,' Craig said. 'You've made him eat a lot of dirt since it happened. His boy's dead. We ought to let him go back. He'll want to be in town when Bud's buried.'

'Orlando, how much dirt has he made you eat in the last five, six years?' Nolan asked.

'Plenty,' Craig said, 'but I've made some money, too. I'm about ready to sell out and leave the county. I don't like to see you break him.'

'That's what I'm going to do,' Nolan said. 'You watch and see. I don't savvy you,

67

Orlando. If he was any kind of a man, you wouldn't have to leave the county. Well, I'm not leaving, and I've eaten all the dirt I aim to. When this is over, Kirk Lamm will be a man you can get along with.'

Craig sighed. 'I'll go talk to him.'

'Suit yourself,' Nolan said. 'If you want to get down on your knees and crawl from here to hellangone just to please Kirk Lamm, it's your business.'

Craig walked across the flat to where Lamm sat. They talked a minute or two, and then Lamm rose and the two men came to the fire. Nolan was eating and didn't look up as Lamm filled a tin plate and poured his coffee.

A few minutes of uneasy silence followed until the men finished supper, then Nolan rolled a cigarette, lighted it with a burning twig from the fire, and rose. He told the others about Zach Grant, and added, 'It's a long shot because I don't think Pony Bartlett is fool enough to let Zach come into camp, but he wanted to try. We're pulling out before dawn, so all of you had better roll in.'

Lamm was on his feet, too, his gaze on Nolan. He said, 'There's something you're not telling us. Why did Grant take that kind of a chance?'

'The reward, Kirk,' Nolan said blandly. 'Maybe I did forget to tell you. You're paying five thousand for information leading

68

to the arrest of the bank robbers and recovery of the money. Now if Grant is real lucky, maybe he'll bring 'em in.'

Lamm's heavy breathing sawed into the brittle stillness, his big face turning almost purple. 'The county will pay that reward,' he said thickly. 'The bank won't.'

'No, the county don't have that big a stake, Kirk,' Nolan said. 'You're the one who's got a real big stake. If you don't get that dinero back, you're busted flat. That's why you're paying the reward.'

'You idiot!' Lamm said in the same, thick-lipped way. 'You stupid fool! You're a part of the company. We're all tied together. So's Orlando here. Why do you insist on me paying when we can make the county do it?'

'We're all tied up together, all right,' Nolan said, 'but it's a funny kind of a knot, now ain't it? Seventy per cent for you and ten per cent for each of us. Well, we've gone along for years, but we got to the end of the road. I'll see that you pay that reward, Kirk, if I have to take it out of the dinero myself.'

Lamm glared at Nolan, so angry he was trembling. Then he could not control himself any longer and he swung a big fist at Nolan's face. He had the ponderous strength of a great ox, but he was slow. Nolan simply pulled his head back so that Lamm's fist didn't quite connect, then he hit the banker on the chin with a sledging, turning fist.

Lamm sprawled on his back, out cold.

Jones and Pratt shook their heads and looked at Nolan with new respect. Craig said, 'You've played hell now, Frank.'

'You expect me to stand here and let him slug me?' Nolan asked. 'He's the one who played hell.'

'I guess he did,' Craig admitted. 'He shouldn't have done what he done, but you pushed him.'

'Pony Bartlett and his friends have been pushed some, too,' Nolan said, 'and now they'll hang. Orlando, did you ever think how it would be to give this county some honest law?'

'Yeah, I've thought of it,' Craig said, his gaze on Lamm.

The banker sat up and shook his head. He started to reach for the gun on his hip, then thought better of it. He got to his feet, staggered a few steps, and went on to the river where he washed his face and then sprawled on his back to stare at the sky. Nolan looked at him and smiled. He was getting his first taste of dirt and he didn't like it.

They let the fire die down, each man making a bed out of his saddle and blanket. Nolan lay awake for a time, staring at the sky, the stars bold and sharp. The breeze, blowing down the canyon, was heavy with pine smell.

When Nolan finally dropped off to sleep, Lamm was sitting across the dying fire from him, a bitter, brooding man. The thought passed through Nolan's mind that the banker might try to kill him during the night, but he dismissed it. Lamm wasn't man enough to try.

He woke during the night and heard the faint sound of gunfire from somewhere up the canyon, then he dropped off again. The next time he woke, the first rosy glow of dawn was in the eastern sky. Clint Jones was building a fire. When Nolan rose and walked toward the river, he wondered if he had dreamed that he had heard shooting during the night. He wheeled and looked at the men who were stirring. Zach Grant was not among them.

CHAPTER EIGHT

Morgan Dillard woke with the first rays of the morning sunlight falling across his bunk from the east window. He thought for a moment that he had not slept at all, then knew that he had. He had stayed awake a long time the previous evening thinking about Mamie Albert and their broken engagement.

He sat up and rubbed his eyes, the

temptation to saddle up and go away riding him hard. He pulled on his pants and boots, built a fire, and, picking up his water bucket, left the cabin. He wondered bleakly how men like Kirk Lamm and Orlando Craig ever got their start. It was all fine and dandy to say they were crooks and worked hand in glove with the sheriff to shape events for their own benefit, but how did they begin?

Maybe it was just the luck of being born in the right family and inheriting money, but he had been fortunate enough to inherit a little. He might as well have thrown it away in a poker game. He guessed that some men like Lamm would have taken the few hundred dollars that his father had left him and built a fortune out of it. Perhaps luck was an element in success, but good judgment was a bigger one, and the brutal truth was his judgment had been bad when he'd bought the Rafter D and mortgaged his future to Kirk Lamm.

He had just passed the haystack on his way to the creek when he heard something rustle in the hay. He stopped and turned, thinking it was probably some ridge runner on his way to Bardo to hide out from the law. If it was, he'd knock the man's teeth out because a fellow like that was likely as not to take a smoke right there in the middle of the stack and start a fire.

Dropping the bucket, he strode to the

72

stack. The hay had been fed until the stack was only about head high. He saw a man's shoulders and grabbed him and hauled him off the top of the stack. He heard a surprised cry, and discovered that it wasn't a man at all. It was a woman, a girl really, slender and attractive, even with the hay in her hair.

Paralyzed by the shock of his discovery, Morgan released his grip just as the girl reached the edge of the stack. She rolled over to the ground and lay on her back looking up at him, her eyes wide with fright. Then the fear seemed to leave her and she smiled at him.

'Hello, Morgan,' she said.

She got to her feet and brushed off some of the hay that clung to her shirt and pants, then turned and picked up a worn Stetson from the stack, putting it on her head. He stared at her, nagged by a feeling he should know her, but not being able to place her. Then, as she swung back toward him, he recognized her.

'You're Laurie, ain't you?' he asked. 'Laurie Jameson?'

'Of course I'm Laurie,' she said. 'I wondered if you knew me.'

'Well, you've grown up,' he said. 'It's been a long time since I saw you. You were just a girl then.'

'I know,' she said. 'Long legs, pigtails down my back, and a lot of freckles. Well,

73

I've still got the freckles and the long legs, but I don't wear my hair in pigtails. I don't wear hay in it usually, either,' she pouted.

'I'm sorry I was rough on you,' he said, 'but all I saw were your shoulders.' Then he stopped. 'Laurie, it just hit me. This is too crazy to be real. What are you doing here, sleeping in my haystack?'

She stood very straight, her eyes on him, her face grave. 'I came here because I didn't know where else to go. I wasn't even sure it was your ranch. When I got here, it was still dark and I didn't want to wake you, so I decided to sleep a little and talk to you when you got up, but I expected to wake up before you did.'

'Why are you here, Laurie?'

She turned to stare at the willows along the creek. She seemed tired and scared and very close to crying, and for a moment he thought he had spoken too sharply to her. Then she looked directly at him again. 'Morgan, I'm putting you in danger. I'm sorry. I wouldn't have done it if I had anywhere else to go, but if you want me to go on and not be a burden to you, just say so.'

'Of course not,' he said impatiently, 'but you still haven't told me why you're here.'

'I ... I ...' She swallowed, then opened her mouth again and this time she got it out. 'I helped rob the Harmony bank yesterday.'

He felt as if she had hit him in the

74

stomach. It was preposterous, unbelievable. She had to be lying, but why? Maybe it was her father who had robbed the bank and she was trying to get the law off his tail. He said curtly, 'Go inside. I'm going after a bucket of water.'

She didn't argue or apologize, but nodded and walked quickly to the cabin and went inside. He stood looking at her, thinking how much she had developed since he had seen her more than four years ago. He remembered she had been a tomboy. She had ridden better than most boys her age, she had loved to hunt and fish, and in Lee Jameson's eyes, she was a boy. At least he acted as if he wanted to ignore the obvious fact that nature had given him a girl.

Morgan strode to the creek, filled the bucket, and returned to the cabin. Maybe she wasn't lying. Nobody was likely to mistake her for a boy now except at a distance, but perhaps Lee Jameson's thinking hadn't changed. If that was the case, he might have had his daughter help him and Pony Bartlett hold up the bank and then told her to ride in one direction while he and Bartlett rode in the other.

Laurie was standing beside the stove when he were in. She said, 'I'm sorry I stopped here. I don't have any right to involve you in my trouble. I'm going on.'

'You're not going on,' he said. 'You sit

75

down over there on the bunk. Or lie down if you want to. I'll fix breakfast. I want to hear what happened. I knew the bank had been robbed and Bud Lamm killed, but that's all.'

He filled the firebox with pine and started coffee. She sat down on the side of the bunk and watched him, so completely worn out that he wondered how she had ever got this far. Finally she said, 'Morgan, you've got a good ranch. When you worked for us, we had a good outfit, too. We had money in the bank and we always had one or two hired hands. Do you have any idea how it is to have everything you owned stolen from you by so-called honest men'

He had started to slice bacon. He stopped to look at her. 'Yes, Laurie, I know exactly how it is. You see, I don't have a good ranch. I'm just about broke. Come fall, Kirk Lamm will take everything I own.'

She was shocked. 'I didn't know. I thought you were doing well.' She swallowed, and then added, 'But you have bacon, Morgan. We've lived on boiled wheat for the last three months. We haven't had any milk or sugar or meat in that time. Pa doesn't even have money to buy shells to shoot jack rabbits.'

'I'm not that bad off.' He finished slicing bacon and put the pan on the stove. 'Why does your pa stay?'

'Because he's stubborn,' she answered. 'Anyhow, he doesn't have any other place to

76

go.'

She paused, staring at her hands that were folded on her lap, then she added, 'There is one reason, Morgan. It won't make good sense to you, but I guess it's the real reason he's stayed. Pa believes in the law. He also believes that in the long run the worthy survive and evil doesn't. He says that sooner or later Kirk Lamm and his friends will be punished and the water will be returned to us.'

'So he lets his family starve while he's waiting for this to happen.' Morgan shook his head. 'It's no good, Laurie. He can't wait that long. Now tell me about the robbery. Was it your pa's way of making the worthy survive?'

'No, no,' she said. 'He wouldn't do anything like that. He doesn't even know I was in it. You see, it was my idea. I went to Pony Bartlett and told him, and then he got Banjo Smith and Doak Watts to help us. My plan was to rob the bank and then tell Lamm he could have the money when he gave our water back to us. Buck Ennis, you know, the stage driver, had told us about a shipment of money that was coming to the bank. He figured there would be about $50,000 in the vault. Lamm had borrowed most of it, so if he lost it, he'd be broke.'

Morgan put a pan of cold biscuits into the oven to warm and set cups and plates and silverware on the table, then took down a jar of honey from a shelf. He said, 'I still don't savvy why you're here.'

'We got out of town all right,' she said, 'and doubled back on the hardpan so they couldn't track us. We camped just below Old Hig's place, and then Pony told me we weren't giving the money back. We'd stick together until we were safe, then we'd split up and each take our share of the money. He had Banjo Smith stand guard while he and Doak slept. I decided I wasn't going to stay with them. I thought Banjo would go to sleep so I could slip out of camp and come here. He stayed awake, but somebody, I guess it was the sheriff or some of his posse, sneaked up the canyon. That was when I got away. There was a lot of shooting and nobody paid any attention to me. I couldn't stay, Morgan. I just couldn't.'

He stood beside the stove waiting for the coffee. He knew now that he would never have any part of the reward. Perhaps it was a greater crime to steal from a bank than it was to steal water; possibly it was a greater crime to shoot and kill Bud Lamm than it was to cause men like Pony Bartlett to turn to bank robbing. Even so, Morgan knew he couldn't bring him self to capture them or even give information about them to a sheriff like Frank Nolan.

He had suffered at Kirk Lamm's hands

and he would suffer more. All he could think of right now was the fact that he had a great deal in common with Pony Bartlett and the others, and so, regardless of how the line ran between the bank robbers and the legal robbers—he felt the term fitted Lamm and Nolan and their friends—he would have nothing to do with capturing them.

'I went to Old Hig's place,' Laurie went on. 'I couldn't take my horse, so I stole Old Hig's gray mare. I rode her bareback to the bottom of the grade and turned her loose. She'll go back.'

The coffee was ready. He poured it and called her to the table, thinking there was more to her reason for leaving Bartlett and the two boys than she had told him, but he didn't want to quiz her. She would tell him what she wanted him to know in her own time.

She ate ravenously, then sat back and yawned. She said, 'I'll go on walking, Morgan. I don't know what possessed me to stop here and get you—'

'Hold it, Laurie,' he said impatiently. 'You're not going on, so stop talking about it. If I have to fight the sheriff and the posse to keep them from taking you, I'll do it. I'll take you home as soon as it's safe. Your folks will be worried.'

'I want to tell you about the robbery if you have time to listen,' she said.

'I've got all the time in the world,' he said. 'I'm not going anywhere today.'

She told him how it had gone, emphasizing what Pony Bartlett had told her about being forced to shoot Bud Lamm. When she was done, he asked, 'Do you think anyone recognized you?'

'I don't know,' she answered. 'Of course we hoped that if anyone saw what happened, they'd take me for a boy. Nobody much was on the street because of the cold wind and the blowing dust. The dust was so thick they couldn't see very well.'

'You lie down and sleep a while,' he said. 'We'll figure out what to do after you wake up.'

'What's going to happen if Pony and the boys come after me?' she asked.

'You'll be safe here,' he said. 'If they stop and ask, I'll say I don't know anything about you.'

'Suppose they insist on looking into the cabin?'

'I won't let them.' He picked up his cup of coffee and sipped it, looking at her over the rim. 'There's one thing I don't savvy. There's no question about who owns the water. Why didn't your pa and his neighbors go to court?'

'They did,' she answered, 'but there's always a question about who owns water if you want to go to court. At least that's what

80

the lawyer in Harmony said. There's only one, Paul Varnum. I guess he came after you left, so maybe you don't know him.'

Morgan shook his head. 'No, I don't.'

'Anyhow, we paid him to start a suit to recover the water. He said we'd win, but it seemed like he wasted a lot of time. After it finally came up before the Judge, he said he'd take it under advisement. Well, that's where it is right now, and we don't have any money to carry it to a higher court if the Judge gives the water to the company. It's too late even if he decides in our favor. We don't have enough money to live on till we get a crop harvested.'

He realized that she had reached the point of exhaustion where she would be sick if she didn't get some sleep. He rose and motioned toward the bunk. 'Go sleep a while. We can't do anything till dark. Might be they're watching us right now. If they ain't, they will be.'

She rose and staggered to the bunk. Sprawled across it, she went to sleep at once. He looked at her for a moment, thinking she had grown up into an attractive woman. One with courage, too. Her idea about the bank money might have worked if Pony Bartlett hadn't turned greedy.

He cleaned up the dishes and laid his rifle and all the .30-.30 shells he had on the table. He buckled his gun belt around him and checked his revolver. The only ammunition he had for the .45 was in the loops of the belt.

One thing was sure, he told himself sourly. He didn't have enough shells to hold out if it came to a siege, and that might happen if Nolan decided to search the cabin. He didn't know what Bartlett and the boys would do, but it didn't seem logical that they would want Laurie bad enough to fight for her.

He went outside and cut wood for a time, keeping one eye on the trail where it came out of the timber near the mouth of Short Creek. Half an hour later he saw three riders splash across the stream and head toward his cabin. Quickly, he gathered an armload of wood and carried it inside, then picked up his rifle and moved to the doorway. When the three men reached the cabin, he stepped outside and pulled the door shut.

'Howdy, Morgan,' Bartlett said.

'Howdy, Pony.'

Morgan nodded at the boys, remembering that they had been in their middle teens when he had seen them last. Now they were grown, but still boys in the sense that they lacked the lean toughness which characterized Pony Bartlett. He looked much older than Morgan remembered him.

For a time they were silent, Bartlett studying Morgan, then he said, 'You got somebody in the cabin you don't want us to see?'

'That's right,' Morgan said. 'It's my business who she is.'

'Well now,' Bartlett said, 'maybe she belongs to me. If she does...'

'No, she's from down Peace Creek a ways,' Morgan said. 'The point is my girl,' he motioned toward the Albert ranch, 'don't know about this one and I don't aim for you or nobody else to tell her. I heard about the bank robbery, Pony. That's something else. I ain't getting into trouble on account of it.'

Bartlett scratched a leathery cheek. 'Maybe you got fifty thousand dollars in that cabin along with a girl.'

'What in the hell are you talking about?' Morgan demanded. 'I never saw that kind of money in my life.'

'Laurie Jameson helped us hold up the bank,' Bartlett said. 'Last night she ran off with the dinero. We're going to get it back. If you're hiding her and the money, you're in trouble, Morgan. Bad trouble. We'll be back if we don't find her. You can count on that.'

He turned his horse and rode up Peace Creek toward Bardo, the other two following. Morgan stared after them wondering if Laurie had lied, or if Bartlett had. If it was Laurie, she was taking him for a sucker and he didn't like the notion a little bit.

CHAPTER NINE

Morgan went back into the cabin and closed and barred the door. He crossed the room to the bunk and stood looking down at Laurie. She lay on her side, one hand under her cheek, her breasts rising and falling in the regular rhythm of breathing. He found it hard to believe she'd had any part in holding up a bank. Now, looking at her this way, he saw her as the child she had been when he'd worked for her father, and knew at once that was foolish.

Laurie Jameson was a woman eighteen years old, a courageous woman who had thought of a way to strike back at Kirk Lamm and the rest of the Harmony bunch and, having thought of it, had the toughness to do something about it. He was sure, even before he heard what she had to say she'd had good reason for whatever she had done.

Reaching down, Morgan gripped a shoulder and shook her awake. She protested in a sleepy grumble and pulled away from him, but he shook her again and this time her eyes came open.

'Can't you let a girl sleep?' she asked. 'Is the house on fire?'

'That's right,' he said. 'The house is on fire, the redcoats are coming, and the sheriff

84

is outside looking for a pretty girl and fifty thousand dollars.'

Laurie had shut her eyes, but now she opened one of them. For a moment she didn't move, then she sat up and rubbed her eyes. She got up and staggered across the room to the bench that held the wash basin and a bucket of water. She poured water into the basin and washed her face, then dried herself on the towel that hung by the door and turned to face Morgan.

'I know you're not a mean man,' she said, 'but it would take a mean man to wake me up without having a good reason.'

'I've got plenty of reason,' Morgan said. 'Pony Bartlett and the other two were here while ago looking for you and the bank money. Bartlett claims you ran off last night with the dinero. That ain't exactly the way you tell it.'

She pulled a bench back from the table and sat down. She stared at Morgan, wide-eyed, then she asked, 'You think I lied to you?'

'Either you or Bartlett lied,' he said. 'I figure you had plenty of reason to lie if you did, but I've got a right to know.'

'Why?'

Exasperated, he said, 'Laurie, you may not know it, but you're in a hell of a tight spot. You've got three outlaws hunting you to get the fifty thousand back if Pony told the truth, and you're gonna have the sheriff and a posse looking for you before dark. You're in trouble if either one catch you. I figure I can help you and I will because I owe that much to your pa, but like I said, I've got a right to know the truth.'

'All right,' she said. 'I'm in a tight spot and I don't mind telling you the truth, though how you can help me is more than I know. I took the money and I hid it. I acted in good faith, but Pony and Banjo and Doak didn't. I'll see that the bank gets the money when water is running in the Dry Fork canal again and they give us some assurance it will keep on running.'

Morgan nodded, not at all sure she could ever bargain with Kirk Lamm and his partners, but it was worth a try. As she said, she had acted in good faith. Maybe, if she could hold out long enough, she could bargain with Lamm. One thing was sure. The loss of that much money was bound to hurt the banker, perhaps even destroy him.

'You can't stay here,' he said. 'I told you we wouldn't move till dark, but we've got to take a chance. Bartlett said they'd be back if they didn't find you, and I don't suppose I'd have a chance keeping the posse from searching the cabin. It looks to me like our best bet is to get you out of here now.'

'I'm not going home,' she said with finality. 'You might just as well forget it if

86

that was what you—'

'It wasn't,' he broke in. 'We'd be sure to run into somebody we didn't want to meet before we got over the pass. Right now I'm taking you to my neighbors, the Alberts. I think they'll keep you till dark and by that time we'll figure out something else. Maybe we'll ride down Peace Creek and keep on going. I dunno. The only thing I'm sure of right now is that we can't get out and travel while it's daylight.'

Her hands were on her lap closing and opening and closing again. The pulse in her forehead was pounding hard. Watching her while she thought this over, Morgan sensed the tension that gripped her. She had to trust him because there was no one else she could trust. He wondered if Pony Bartlett had any idea what he had done to the girl.

'I've never seen the Alberts,' Laurie said finally, 'but if you think they'll hide me, we'll go there. I suppose there's a reward for my arrest and if they're like most people, they'd turn me over for part of it.'

'We won't tell them you had anything to do with the robbery,' Morgan said. 'I'll think of a lie they'll believe. I'll saddle up and you can ride behind me.' He turned to the door, lifted the bar, then looked back over his shoulder. 'I know we're taking a chance if we leave the cabin, but it's a smaller risk than staying here.'

He went out, shutting the door behind him. As he crossed the yard to the corral, he looked at the mountains, particularly studying the opening in the timber that the road made as it came down from the pass. Seeing nothing that alarmed him, he went on to the corral and saddled his sorrel.

He was playing this blind, but he didn't know any other way he could play it. All he could hope for now was to get Laurie to the Albert place. There would be time later to figure out the next move. He stepped into the saddle and rode to the cabin, still watching the timber. Laurie ran out and swung up behind him, her arms hugging him around the waist.

The ride to Pothook was a short one and took only a few minutes, but it dragged out so that it seemed hours to Morgan. By the time he reached the Albert house, he had thought of a story to tell them. He waited until Laurie had slid to the ground, then he dismounted and tied the sorrel.

'Let me do the lying,' he said. 'You just listen and agree to everything I tell them.'

She nodded, but he saw that she was so exhausted she seemed only half aware of what was going on. The short sleep she'd had this morning had not rested her. He could only hope that Mamie and her mother would let Laurie sleep.

They walked up the path to the front door.

Morgan knocked. Mamie opened the door immediately and smiled as she said, 'Come in.' She had seen them come, Morgan thought. If she was surprised to see him ride up with a strange girl in a little over twelve hours from the time she had broken her engagement with him, she did not show it.

Morgan introduced them, adding, 'You remember I used to work for the Jamesons in Dry Fork valley before I bought the Rafter D.'

'Why yes, I do remember,' Mamie said.

Mrs Albert came out of the kitchen and Mamie introduced Laurie to her. He said, 'Laurie's in trouble. Her folks are trying to make her marry a man she can't stand. He has a little money and you've heard how it is out there on Poverty Flat. Laurie would do anything to help her folks, I reckon, except marry this fellow.'

'Who is it that wants to marry her?' Mamie asked, glancing obliquely at Morgan and then bringing her gaze back to Laurie's face.

Before Morgan could answer, Laurie said, 'His name is Ackley. Tom Ackley. He's new in the country. I'm sure you never heard of him.'

'What does he do for a living?' Mamie asked.

'He bought the Dry Fork store,' Laurie said.

She was on her toes, Morgan told himself, and realized that he hadn't been very smart. He had not considered the possibility that Mamie would be suspicious enough to ask questions. He had been so intent on getting Laurie out of his cabin and watching the timber for the posse that he hadn't figured out the details of his story.

'Well,' Mamie said, 'if a man who had money wanted to marry me, I'd take him in a minute.'

'Not Tom Ackley.' Laurie sat down and began to cry, then she recovered her self control and wiped her eyes. 'He's a terrible old man. He chews tobacco, he never takes a bath, and he stinks.'

'I should say you wouldn't want to marry a man like that.' Mrs Albert patted Laurie on the back. 'Now let me fix you a cup of tea.'

'She's all in,' Morgan said. 'She rode all night to get over the pass. What she needs is sleep. I wondered if you'd take care of her for a while?'

'Of course we will,' Mrs Albert said. 'Come on, honey. You can sleep in Mamie's bed.'

Laurie rose and Mrs Albert slipped an arm around her. Morgan watched as they crossed the room and disappeared into one of the bedrooms. Mrs Albert was a big, motherly woman who liked and trusted everyone and believed almost anything, but Mamie was different. Morgan turned to her when the bedroom door closed, not at all sure that his idea about bringing Laurie here was a good one.

'I hadn't seen her for four years,' Morgan said. 'She's grown up. She was a tomboy when I worked for her father.'

'She's a woman now,' Mamie said. 'A pretty one, too.'

'I guess that fellow Ackley thought so,' Morgan said. 'Her pa is a hardheaded old boy. When he gets his mind made up, you don't change it. After she ran away, she couldn't think of any place to go except to come to me. I'm pretty sure her pa will figure out where she went and he'll be here looking for her any minute.'

'If she's eighteen, she doesn't have anything to worry about,' Mamie said. 'She looks older, but maybe she isn't.'

'She is eighteen,' Morgan said, 'but it wouldn't make any difference how old she is. You don't know her pa.'

'We'll hide her,' Mamie said. 'Don't worry. He'll never know she's here.'

'I was hoping you'd do that,' Morgan said.

'Sit down.' Mamie motioned to a chair. 'I'll put the coffee pot on. I'm sorry about what I said. I guess my temper just got away from me, but you know how it's been, putting off getting married the way we have.'

'No, I've got to get back,' Morgan said.

'I'll come over this evening and see how Laurie is.'

Mamie laid a hand on his arm, a proprietary gesture as if nothing had happened between them. She said, 'Come for supper.'

He stood motionless, not wanting to come. For a few hours he had felt like a free man who could ride away from all of his obligations. Mamie had broken their engagement and the bank was welcome to take the Rafter D.

Now, looking at Mamie's expectant face, he had a disturbing feeling that she regretted her burst of temper and wanted him back. Well, he wasn't free now. He had Laurie on his hands and he couldn't afford to make Mamie angry.

'I'll be here,' he said, and left the house.

He rode back to his cabin, certain that the posse would be along sometime today. All he could do was to wait. Laurie would be all right, he thought. Then, remembering Mamie's suspicious questions, he wasn't sure.

CHAPTER TEN

A red arc of the sun was barely showing above the eastern horizon when the posse started up the river, Sheriff Frank Nolan leading. The men rode hunched forward in their saddles, coat collars around their throats.

The chill air was penetrating, and the farther they rode toward the pass, the colder the air became. The bottom of the canyon was dark with shadow, the sharp rays of the rising sun striking the upper half of the walls and turning them a fiery red.

The sunlight had not quite reached the bottom of the canyon when they found Zach Grant sitting with his back to a boulder, his long legs stretched out in front of him. His red bandanna was wrapped around his forehead, a streak of dried blood showing on the right side of his face.

'What the hell happened to you?' Nolan asked as he swung to the ground.

'What does it look like?'

'Looks like you got hit.'

'You're looking real good if you can see that,' Grant said sourly. 'Sure took you yahoos a long time to get here.'

The others dismounted and stood looking down at Grant. Craig asked, 'What happened?'

Grant started to say something, but the only sound he made was a long, drawn out grunt. He ran the tip of his tongue over dry, cracked lips. Nolan motioned to Pratt. 'Give him a drink, Simon.'

Pratt handed his canteen to Grant who took a long swallow, then swished another mouthful from one side to the other and spat it out. 'Thanks,' he said. 'I sure was spitting cotton. I tried to get down to the creek while ago, but I fell flat on my face. I feel better now. I think I can ride if one of you will fetch my horse.' He motioned downstream. 'I left him down there a piece.'

'Go get him, Kirk,' Nolan said.

For a moment Lamm faced the sheriff, his legs spread, his face dark with fury, but it lasted only a moment. He wheeled away from Nolan and started downstream.

The sheriff laughed softly. 'He sure don't like to take orders. Trouble with him is he's been giving 'em too long.'

'Damn it, Frank,' Craig said irritably, 'you keep pushing. Let up on him.'

'Oh no,' Nolan said. 'I told you he was gonna eat dirt and he's gonna keep on eating it. There's just one thing you can count on, Orlando. When we get back to Harmony, nothing is gonna be the same.'

'I can believe it,' Craig said, staring at Lamm's broad back as he worked his way downstream through the boulders.

'All right, Zach,' Nolan said. 'Now tell us what happened.'

Grant rose and stood with his back against the boulder. He raised a hand to the side of his head, felt of it gingerly, and grinned a little. 'I ran into a buzzsaw. That's what happened. I seen their campfire up the canyon a piece, so I tied my horse and started toward it, figuring I could take 'em if I surprised 'em, or maybe holler at 'em and palaver with 'em if they had a guard out. I thought I was moving quiet like, but they musta heard me. All of a sudden they started shooting, so I got down behind them rocks yonder.'

He motioned toward a nest of boulders in front of him. 'I was purty close to 'em, but it was darker'n the inside of a bull's gut. I couldn't see nothing but their campfire. Might have been a bunch of ghosts shooting at me. I shot back a few times, but I don't reckon I hit any of 'em. All I wanted was to keep 'em up there. Dark as it was they could of sneaked down the canyon and put a knife into me afore I knowed they was here.'

'How many do you figure were shooting at you?' Nolan asked.

Grant took another drink from the canteen and shook his head. 'I dunno, Sheriff. No way to tell. Seemed like a dozen, as much lead as they was throwing at me, but there couldn't have been more'n four. I dunno what happened after I got hit. I was out cold. Why they didn't come on down and beef me is something I dunno.'

'Running is all they're thinking about,' Nolan said.

Lamm was back then with Grant's horse. He handed the reins to Grant, his hard stare boring into Nolan. 'I did what you told me to,' he said, and turned to his mount.

Grant took one step forward and would have fallen if he hadn't been close enough to the horse to grab the horn. He stood motionless a moment, his eyes closed, then he lifted a foot to the stirrup and swung into the saddle. He sat there, biting his lower lip. His head must be feeling as if it was going to explode, Nolan thought.

'You'll feel better after while,' Nolan said. 'At least that's been my experience. If you can hang and rattle for maybe an hour, the worst will wear off.'

'It's got to,' Grant said. 'It can't get no worse.'

'We'll ride on up the canyon and talk to Old Hig,' Nolan said. 'They might have gone in any direction, but I still think they'll go over the pass and either hide out in the lava or go up Peace Creek to Bardo. If you're not any better, Zach, we'll leave you with Old Hig.'

'The hell you will,' Grant said. 'That old bastard would stick a knife between my ribs before you were out of sight. He don't like me no better'n I like him.'

'You want to go back to town?' Nolan asked.

'No,' Grant said. 'I can stand it. I just ain't

96

gonna do no fancy riding.'

'Doc Vance ought to look at him,' Craig said. 'A head wound like that can be dangerous.'

'I'm all right, damn it,' Grant said stubbornly. 'Light out. I'll just take it slow.'

Nolan mounted and rode upstream, grinning a little as he saw that the others kept some distance behind him. There was a chance they'd run into an ambush and all six of them might be cut down before they had a chance to reach cover, but he was gambling on his hunch that the outlaws were on the run and had no intention of doing anything else.

His hunch seemed to be correct. They reached Old Hig's place without trouble. He had a solid log cabin on the very top of the pass, the ground sloping away on all sides. There was no timber within one hundred yards of his house, so he could see a man coming from any direction.

Nolan glanced at the barn that was located below the house. Craig was the closest to him and he was at least fifty yards back down the road. Nolan dismounted beside the barn and waited until the others came up.

'You're a brave posse,' he jeered. 'I guess you figure that I'm welcome to stop any lead that's flying around and you'll have time to get back into the timber.'

'That's right,' Craig said. 'You're the one

who's sure they're on down the mountain by now and heading for the lava bed.'

'I'm the one,' Nolan said. 'If Zach's noggin wasn't hurting like the devil, he'd be up here with me, but the rest of you are just plain yellow.'

'Go ahead and insult us,' Clint Jones snapped. 'That don't make us hanker to get our heads shot off.'

Grant eased out of the saddle, then stood beside his horse for a moment, one hand gripping the horn. He said, 'I'm feeling better, Sheriff. I think I can walk from here to the barn door, open it, and see who's inside. I'd say nobody else in this here posse but you has got the guts to do it.'

Nolan laughed softly as he dismounted. 'You're right, Zach. Let's you and me see if they are holed up inside.'

The sheriff drew his revolver, opened the barn door, and went in. He walked behind the half dozen stalls, noting that one held a gray mare, one a bony bay gelding that was Old Hig's pack animal, and that the other four were empty. The north half of the barn was the hay mow. The hay was nearly gone, and Nolan wondered what the old man would do until the grass was up. Hay was expensive and hard to get, and Old Hig never seemed to have much money.

As Nolan turned and walked back along the runway, the thought occurred to him that Old Hig might have more money than anyone in Harmony guessed. He never spent much, and he wasn't one to put his money in a bank. He probably had buried it somewhere around his house.

Grant remained inside the doorway, his revolver in one hand, the other braced against the wall. 'Nothing here just like we thought,' he said.

'That's right.' Nolan shut the door as Grant staggered to his horse and mounted. 'We'll talk to Old Hig, but I don't figure he'll tell us anything.'

'He'll tell us if he knows,' Grant said ominously. 'I've waited years for this chance and I sure ain't gonna miss out on it now.'

Nolan mounted and led the posse up the slope toward the house, glancing at Grant's face. He had not realized until that moment how great was the man's hatred for Old Hig. It was probably this hatred which had kept Grant in the saddle for the last hour when the sheer agony of riding had been enough to make a lesser man faint. Then he thought with some surprise that this was exactly the way he felt about Kirk Lamm.

Higgins was standing on the porch watching them ride up the hill. He was a very old man. No one as far as Nolan knew had any idea how old he really was. He was all hide and bone, with long white hair and a white beard. One hand gripped a porch post above his head, the other hung at his side. They were big-knuckled, the backs of both covered by dark liver spots. At one time he must have been a large, very strong man, but that had been before Frank Nolan's day.

'Howdy,' Old Hig said. 'What brings you boys out so early in the morning?'

'We're after the outlaws who held up Lamm's bank,' Grant said. 'We think you know where they are.'

Nolan was surprised that Grant assumed the responsibility of questioning Higgins, but he was even more surprised at the blank expression on the old man's face.

'Well, I sure don't,' Higgins said. 'All I can tell you is that somebody must have stole my gray mare last night and rode her a spell. I ain't real sure even about that, but she came up the trail from Peace Creek this morning. Whoever rode her didn't bother with the saddle.'

Grant swung down and stood motionless until his head cleared, then he moved forward and stepped up on the porch to stand beside Old Hig. He said, 'You're lying. They're your friends from Poverty Flat. You'll tell us where they are or I'll beat your guts out.'

'I can't tell you something I don't know,' Old Hig said.

'Wait, Zach,' Nolan called. 'They might be in the house. Take a look, Kirk.'

100

Lamm hesitated, giving Nolan his black, bitter look, but he dismounted without argument and went into the house. He came back a moment later and mounted. He said, 'Empty.'

'All right, Higgins,' Grant said. 'Where are they?'

'Damn it, I don't know,' the old man said angrily. 'I told—'

Grant slugged him on the side of the head, knocking him off the porch onto the ground. He got up slowly as Grant stepped off the porch. He tried to hit Grant, but he was slow. Grant struck him again, this time in the belly. Higgins went down a second time and lay motionless, unable to breathe for a moment.

'That's enough,' Craig said. 'What's the matter with you, Frank? You going to let that crazy fool kill Old Hig?'

'It wouldn't be much loss,' Nolan said. 'There's a chance the old bastard does know where they went.'

'I never knew you had a mean streak in you like this,' Craig said as he drew his gun. 'Grant, if you touch him again, I'll blow your head off.'

Grant had kicked Higgins in the ribs. He started to draw his foot back to kick the old man again, but he put it down. He asked, 'Sheriff, who's running this shebang?'

Nolan laughed. 'Well, sir, Zach, some

strange things come out on a hunt like this. Kirk takes orders like a good little boy. Orlando turns out to have a weak stomach, and you show us you're a ring-tailed wowser. Well, I guess you've had your fun. Mount up.'

'I just started on this old...'

'Get on your horse,' Nolan said. 'Hig, if you're lying, you're a dead man.'

Grant mounted reluctantly as Nolan wheeled his horse and rode down the slope. The rest followed, Craig in the rear, his gaze on Old Hig who had pulled himself into an upright position and sat with a hand over his belly.

Nolan glanced up at the sun, thinking it was a long ride down the west side of the pass to Peace Creek. They wouldn't tackle the lava beds until they had to. If Morgan Dillard couldn't tell them anything about the outlaws, they'd check with Mike Twill in Bardo. If he couldn't help, the hunt would be long and possibly futile.

A small grin curled the corners of Frank Nolan's mouth. He didn't really care how the chase turned out as long as he broke Kirk Lamm.

CHAPTER ELEVEN

Morgan spent the remainder of the morning and the early part of the afternoon cleaning out the corral, a chore he had been putting off for weeks. As he worked, he watched the opening in the timber on the other side of Peace Creek where the road leveled off below the pass. Presently the posse appeared as he knew it would.

Leaving the wheelbarrow outside the corral gate, he picked up his Winchester and returned to the cabin. He expected the posse to come to the cabin immediately, but he was surprised to see two men dismount and examine the road. One of them walked about fifty feet up the creek toward Bardo, his gaze on the road. Then he turned and joined the others. They talked for a time, then the two men on the ground mounted and all six rode toward Morgan's cabin.

He recognized Kirk Lamm's squat, thick body first, then Frank Nolan who was in the lead, and before they reached him, he made out Orlando Craig, Simon Pratt, and Clint Jones. The sixth man wore a bandanna around his head. He looked familiar, and Morgan knew he had seen him around Harmony, but it took a moment to place him, then he remembered.

The man was Zach Grant, a hunter and trapper and guide who had the reputation of being a tough hand. Grant and the sheriff belonged in a posse, but it struck Morgan that the others didn't. He stared at them when they reined up in front of him, making no effort to hide his hostility, his gaze finally coming to rest on Kirk Lamm. The banker looked as if he had been whipped; the overbearing insolence that had always been a part of him was gone. The mighty had fallen, Morgan told himself.

'Howdy,' Nolan said finally. 'I haven't seen you for a spell, Dillard.'

'I haven't seen you, either, Sheriff,' Morgan said sharply, 'but I've seen your banker friend real recent. If he fetched you along to foreclose on me, you can get to hell out of here.'

'Hold it, son, hold it,' Nolan said. 'You just grabbed the wrong bull by the tail. Kirk's bank was robbed and we're after the outlaws. We thought you could help us.'

'Sure,' Morgan jeered. 'I've got 'em hid in the house.'

'Maybe we'd better look,' Nolan said as he swung down.

'Got a search warrant?' Morgan demanded.

The sheriff dropped the reins to the ground and took a step toward Morgan, then stopped. 'Why no, we don't,' he admitted, 'but I figured you were the kind of man who would cooperate with the law.'

'I'll cooperate with the law, all right.' Morgan jabbed a forefinger at Kirk Lamm. 'But I don't feel much like cooperating with that bastard. He turned me down for a loan, so I've got no reason to be friendly to him. If you tore his heart out, you'd find it all twisted up into the shape of a dollar sign.'

Nolan laughed and turned to Lamm. 'He's sure got you sized up, Kirk. You and Simon go take a look in the barn. I don't think Dillard is going to give us any trouble. Fact is, I expect him to invite us into the house for a cup of coffee.' He turned to face Morgan. 'How about it?'

'Sure,' Morgan said. 'Just so long as your fat friend stays outside. I don't mind telling you that I hope the outlaws get away and the bank's busted flat.'

Nolan laughed again. 'My fat friend! You hear that, Kirk?'

Lamm and Pratt were already headed toward the barn. The banker did not look back. Morgan said, 'Come on in,' and led the way into his cabin. It was working out about right, he thought. He wanted to play it tough, but not too tough. The only thing he was really concerned about was keeping their minds off Laurie. He wasn't even sure they knew she was involved in the holdup. He wanted to find out, but he didn't know how

105

to ask without making them suspicious.

The four men followed him inside, Nolan's gaze sweeping the interior of the cabin. There wasn't even a closet in the big room that could hide a man. Morgan poured the coffee and handed the tin cups to the men, saying, 'I didn't expect any company, so it's lucky I didn't throw the coffee out. I usually do unless I'm looking for Steve Albert to drop in.'

Nolan sipped his coffee, his gaze on Morgan. He said, 'Dillard, as far as I know, you've never been in trouble with the law. I reckon you don't want to be now.'

'If Kirk Lamm's the law—' Morgan began.

'He's not,' Nolan cut in sharply. 'I am, and don't you forget it. All I want to tell you is that the folks on Smoky River have their cash deposited in Lamm's bank. If he doesn't get this money back, he's broke, the bank closes its doors, and a lot of good people lose everything they have.'

'Pony Bartlett's lost everything already,' Morgan said. 'Maybe he was justified in robbing the bank.'

'How do you know he did?' Nolan asked.

'He said he did, him and Banjo Smith and Doak Watts.'

'When?'

'This morning. They stopped here after coming over the pass. They were headed up Peace Creek toward Bardo.' He glanced at

106

Orlando Craig and Clint Jones. 'I doubt you'll take them three with the posse you've got, though.'

Zach Grant snickered, then put a hand to the side of his head. 'I ought to know better'n to laugh. I've got enough of a headache from riding that damned horse.' He looked at Nolan. 'He sure called it, Sheriff. I never seen a posse like this one before.'

Nolan was watching Morgan closely. Now he said, 'You used to work for Jameson out on the Dry Fork. I guess you knew his girl Laurie.'

'Sure, I knew her,' Morgan said casually. 'She was just a kid. Why?'

'Are you sure she wasn't with them three bank robbers you talked to this morning?'

'Of course I'm sure,' Morgan said. 'Why should she be with 'em?'

Nolan put his cup down. 'No reason, maybe.'

'We're wasting time, Sheriff,' Grant said. 'I read the sign. What he says fits what I seen. Them bank robbers are in Bardo by now.'

'Yeah, maybe they are.' Nolan turned to the door, then stopped and slowly swung around to face Morgan. 'Why did they stop here? It would have made more sense for 'em to head upstream for Bardo the minute they came down off the pass. Strikes me that

107

maybe they came here looking for Laurie. Or maybe to leave her with you.'

'If they was looking for her, they didn't say anything about it to me,' Morgan said. 'As for leaving her with me, you can have her if you can find her. I can't.'

'He ain't hid her in here,' Grant said. 'Come on, let's ride.'

'Maybe they didn't go as far as Bardo,' Morgan said. 'They didn't tell me their plans. Could be they went up Peace Creek, then circled around to the lava beds. If they did, you'll be a long time running 'em down.'

'I reckon so,' Nolan said. 'If you knew they had held up the bank, why did you give 'em any grub?'

'Pony Bartlett was my friend when I worked for Jameson,' Morgan answered. He paused, staring through the open doorway at Kirk Lamm who had returned from the barn with Pratt, then he added angrily, 'You know how I feel about that bastard. Why shouldn't I help a man who had robbed him? Maybe you'd like for me to tell you what Lamm said when I asked for a loan?'

'No, I can guess,' Nolan said. 'I don't have time to bother with you now, but we'll be back. By your own admission you aided and abetted men you knew were criminals. That's enough to send you to Canon City for a good stretch.'

Nolan strode out of the cabin, mounted, and rode back the way he had come, the others following. Morgan watched until the six men disappeared up the creek toward Bardo. He picked up his Winchester and crossed the yard to the corral, not at all sure he had played this right. He wasn't sure, either, whether Laurie had been positively identified as one of the bank robbers.

He pushed the wheelbarrow into the corral, thinking that Laurie was the only one who knew where the money was. That meant Pony Bartlett and the two boys would be back looking for her, and if the posse didn't catch the three bank robbers, it would be back.

Sooner or later one bunch or the other would think of checking with the Alberts. He had to get her out of the Albert house as soon as it was dark. It was a good thing he had taken her there, but it was no final solution to their problem. He glanced worriedly at the sun, thinking he might not have until dark.

CHAPTER TWELVE

Late in the afternoon Morgan saddled his sorrel and rode to the Albert place. It had been a draggy afternoon, with uneasiness plaguing him until he could not stand it any longer. Now that he was here at the Albert ranch, he wasn't sure he should have come this early. Glancing at the sun, he saw it was still two hours before dark.

Mamie came down the path to meet him. She kissed him, then put an arm around his waist as they walked toward the house. He wanted to push her arm away, to tell her she had broken the engagement and that was the end of it. When he looked at her, only half listening to her chatter, he sensed that as far as Mamie was concerned, they were still engaged. She expected him to accept what she had said just before he'd left, that she had let her temper get away from her, that she was sorry she had said what she had, but he knew how it was, putting off their marriage the way they had.

Well, he couldn't accept it. He was satisfied to leave the engagement broken, but there was Laurie. For the time being at least he had to be decently courteous to Mamie because he couldn't have her calling up someone in Harmony and saying that one of the bank robbers was here. Not that the Alberts knew Laurie had anything to do with the holdup, but they might get suspicious.

They went into the front room, Mamie saying, 'Sit down, Morgan. Supper's almost ready.'

Mrs Albert came out of the kitchen,

wiping her hands on her apron. 'I hope you're good and hungry, Morgan. Mamie baked a chocolate cake and I think she got a good do on it.'

'I'm hungry enough,' Morgan said.

Mamie and her mother disappeared into the kitchen. Steve walked into the front room, nodding as he asked, 'How are you tonight, Morgan?'

'Fine.'

He didn't see Laurie and he wondered if she was still asleep. He rolled a cigarette and lighted it, the sense of uneasiness growing in him until he found it hard to breathe. Steve sat down. His face had a scrubbed look about it; his iron-gray hair had been recently combed.

Something was wrong. Morgan couldn't identify the reason for the feeling, but the Albert family was normally not sly or devious about anything, and right now Morgan felt they were hiding something. There was a strange cat-and-mouse atmosphere here that wasn't natural. He knew he might be imagining it because he was worried about Laurie, not knowing what he was going to do with her, and he also knew he was irritated by Mamie's taking him for granted. Still the feeling persisted.

'How's Laurie?' Morgan asked after a moment's silence.

'Fine. Ma just woke her up a little while

111

ago.' Steve cleared his throat, giving Morgan a searching glance, then he asked, 'Hear anything more about the bank robbers?'

'No.'

'I saw you had some visitors this afternoon.'

Morgan nodded. 'It was the sheriff and his posse. They wanted to know if I'd seen the bank robbers.'

'Did you?'

'Yeah, they came by this morning. I talked to Pony Bartlett, then they rode up the creek toward Bardo. That was all I could tell Nolan.'

'That so?' Steve raised his eyebrows as if to say there was more he could have told, then the temptation was too great for him to turn down, and he blurted, 'Well now, you could have said that you know—'

'Pa.' Mamie yelled the word at him, then she seemed to realize she should not have spoken that way. 'I'm sorry, but when you get to talking, you can't hear it thunder. I declare, Morgan, we're going to have to get him an ear trumpet. Come on now. Supper's ready.'

Steve's face turned red. 'We're coming, we're coming,' he said, and got up.

Morgan followed them into the kitchen. Laurie stood at the stove stirring a pan of gravy. She looked over her shoulder at Morgan and smiled. Her eyes were still red from sleep and he thought she looked tired.

'Get rested?' he asked.

'Oh yes,' Laurie answered. 'I feel good.'

'The gravy's ready, looks like,' Mrs Albert said. 'Here, you can pour it into this dish.'

Laurie obeyed and carried the bowl to the table. They sat down and began to eat, talking very little at first until the sharp edge of their appetites had been blunted. This was the way it usually went when Morgan ate with the Alberts. They were all good eaters and were always more interested in food than conversation until the dessert came.

Mamie brought the chocolate cake to the table and everybody admired it. Mrs Albert sliced it and passed it, then Mamie said, 'Morgan, if the posse catches the outlaws in Bardo, I guess you'll get the reward.'

Morgan shot a glance at Laurie. She was helping herself to the cake and acted as if she hadn't heard. The Alberts had ignored her through the first part of the meal, and they ignored her now except for Mamie who took the cake plate when she passed it.

'No, I wouldn't get all of it,' Morgan said. 'The posse members would get some.'

'If we get it,' Mamie began, paused, and finally went on, 'I mean, if you got it, our financial problem would be solved, wouldn't it?'

Mamie smiled as she passed the cake to

her mother. The inference was clear, Morgan thought. He had told her they couldn't get married as long as he was in debt the way he was, but he could use the reward money to pay the bank off. He would have no reason, then, for not marrying her.

'I'm afraid it wouldn't be enough,' he said. 'There were six men in the posse. When you divide the reward money up, it wouldn't amount to much for any of us.'

'Well,' Mamie said. 'I guess we can claim one full fourth. They'd have the other three-fourths to divide. We'd have part of that, too, with you telling the posse that the outlaws had gone to Bardo.'

Morgan put his fork down, his heart hammering. He knew now why he had sensed that something was wrong. The cat-and-mouse feeling was exactly right. The Alberts were playing cat-and-mouse with him and Laurie.

'How do you figure we'd have one full fourth?' Morgan asked, his gaze on Mamie.

He knew what she would say, but he wanted to hear her say it. She did, her eyes meeting his. 'Pa called Harmony after you left this afternoon. They told him Miss Jameson was identified as a member of the outlaw band that held the bank up. All we have to do is to turn her over to the sheriff. He'll probably make her tell him where the others went if he hasn't found them. Maybe she knows what happened to the money and he—'

'Oh, no.' Laurie was staring at Mamie, her eyes filled with outrage. 'I wouldn't tell them anything. They'll never get that money if they won't turn the water back into the Dry Fork canal.' She turned to Morgan. 'You brought me here to hold me for the sheriff, didn't you? You're after the reward, too. I hate you. I don't know why I ever trusted you.'

'You see?' Mamie said in triumph. 'One-fourth of five thousand is...'

'Oh, shut up, Mamie,' Morgan said angrily. 'I didn't think you'd do a thing like this. I know what the Dry Fork people have been up against. I'll do all I can to help Laurie until she can work a deal with Kirk Lamm and his bunch for the water. They're our kind of people, but the Harmony bunch ain't. They're bigger robbers than Pony Bartlett ever was.'

'Well now, you just hold on,' Steve said. 'You can't expect us to get on the wrong side of the law hiding a bank robber. It don't make no difference if she is a woman. She's going to jail.'

Mamie was staring at Morgan as if she could not believe what she had heard him say. 'You are a damn fool, Morgan Dillard,' she said shrilly. 'We need that money to get married. You told me so yourself, but now

115

you're throwing it down a rat hole. You're making yourself an outlaw by protecting a bank-robbing murderess. If you go through with what you said, we're finished.'

He stared back at Mamie, thinking he had never really known her. She had always been a pleasant, smiling woman, doing her best to make herself desirable, but now she was another person, hateful and greedy and lacking any sense of justice for Laurie's people who had been almost destroyed by Kirk Lamm and his friends.

'We're finished, all right.' Morgan rose, his fists clenched. 'We were finished when you broke the engagement. We should have been finished a long time ago.'

'I'm going to phone Harmony right now,' Mamie cried. 'I'll tell them you've turned outlaw, trying to hide the bank robbers.'

She jumped up and ran to the phone. As she started to ring, Morgan said, 'Come on, Laurie. We've been here too long now.'

'You're not taking her,' Steve bellowed. 'She's our prisoner. She's worth a lot of money to us. I'm gonna hold her till the sheriff gets here.'

Steve wheeled toward the Winchester that hung on an antler rack near the back door. Morgan grabbed him by the shoulders and whirled him around. He said, 'Steve, you and me have been neighbors for four years. We've never had any trouble. We've never even had angry words, but by God, if you make a move to keep Laurie, I'll beat you to death.'

Steve wilted under his hard stare. He licked his lips, he tried to hold his shoulders back and to clench his fists, but he failed. All he could do was to say in a hoarse voice, 'Get out.'

Laurie had already gone through the front door. Morgan ran after her, untied his horse, and mounted. Laurie swung up behind him and he wheeled the sorrel toward the wall of quaking asps across Peace Creek.

'Hang on,' Morgan said, and put the horse into a run.

The sun was almost down behind the western ridges, but the light was strong enough for them to be seen by riders coming down the creek. Morgan could not see anyone upstream from them. The posse had had time to reach Bardo and return, and Morgan was afraid that they might be back in time to see him and Laurie ride across the meadow.

They splashed through the water and a moment later disappeared into the quakies. He pulled up and let the sorrel pick his way through the trees until he was sure they were out of sight of anyone watching from the meadows or the road that ran along the west bank of the stream, then he pulled up.

Laurie slid to the ground. Morgan

117

dismounted and patted the neck of the heaving animal. When he turned to the girl, he saw she was pale and trembling. She put her hands on his arms. 'Morgan, I apologize for what I said back there. I don't know why I said it.'

'Forget it,' he said. 'We were all snapping at each other. I've got you to thank for getting me away from Mamie. She's a possessive woman. She gave me my walking papers yesterday and then wanted to take them back.'

'Then you're not mad at me because I broke you two up?'

'Mad?' He laughed shortly. 'I'm thankful.'

'What are we going to do now? She will call Harmony.'

'The sheriff ain't there,' he said, 'but he'll be here before long if I'm guessing right. They'll pick up our trail.'

He stared at the sky through the trees. Thinking it would be dark before long. If he had a chance to talk to Nolan, he'd see if they could make some kind of deal for the water and get Laurie off the hook at the same time, but he couldn't let Laurie go to jail where they could pressure her into telling what had happened to the money.

'I still don't know what we're going to do,' Laurie said. 'I guess I have made an outlaw out of you like they said, and I didn't want to do that.'

118

'I'm going to take you to Old Hig's place,' he said. 'It ain't a good idea to keep running. We can't go to my place and you can't go home. I can't think of anything else to do. If Old Hig will hide you, I'll try to find Nolan and talk to him.'

'I don't want to get you into trouble,' she said. 'Or Old Hig, either.'

'I was in trouble the minute Kirk Lamm turned me down on that loan I asked for,' he said. 'Now I'm hoping I can make some trouble for him.'

CHAPTER THIRTEEN

Morgan and Laurie reached Old Hig's place on the summit near midnight. They had kept off the road, so the going had been slow and tiring. Morgan sensed that the girl was completely worn out, but she kept a firm grip around his waist and she never complained.

More than once they had heard horses on the road. Morgan had no way of knowing whether they belonged to the posse or the bank robbers, but it didn't make much difference. One bunch was about as dangerous to him and Laurie as the other.

Once they glimpsed a campfire below them, but again there was no way of determining whether it belonged to the posse or the outlaws. Morgan guessed it was the posse because he was sure Pony Bartlett was smart enough not to build a fire, but the two boys might not be, and it was possible that Bartlett and the boys had separated.

Now, reining up in the shadow of Old Hig's barn, Morgan dismounted and led his horse inside. He tied him in a stall and loosened the cinch. He didn't want anyone prowling around the cabin to find a saddled horse standing outside. There was a good chance that Pony Bartlett or the boys, or all three, would be prowling around here before dawn.

Morgan pulled his Winchester from the boot and, stepping outside, closed the door. Laurie was waiting for him. She said, 'I don't think we ought to just walk up to his door and knock. He's a light sleeper, and if he's had any trouble because of the holdup, he might start shooting before he knows who we are.'

That was true, Morgan thought. Bartlett and the boys might have done their prowling already, thinking that Laurie could have hidden the money in Old Hig's cabin and they'd better make the old man hand it over before the posse got here.

'I'll holler at him,' Morgan said, and raised his voice to shout, 'Hig, we want to talk to...'

A rifle cracked from the cabin before

Morgan could finish, powderflame slashing its red tongue into the darkness, the bullet snapping over their heads. Morgan grabbed Laurie and lunged around the corner of the barn as a second shot sounded, the slug slapping into the log wall waist high where Morgan had been standing a moment before.

'Stop shooting, you idiot,' Morgan yelled. 'We're here to talk, not fight.'

'Talk and be damned,' Old Hig shouted, and fired again.

'Tell him who we are,' Laurie said.

'I'm Morgan Dillard,' Morgan shouted. 'I've got Laurie Jameson with me. We want to talk.'

'Yeah, you're the angel Gabriel and you've got both Mary and Martha,' Old Hig jeered, and threw another shot at them.

'The crazy old fool,' Morgan said in exasperation. 'He'll never believe me. See if he recognizes your voice.'

'Hig, this is Laurie Jameson,' the girl shouted. 'You know my voice, don't you?'

Old Hig didn't say anything or shoot for what must have been a full minute, although to Morgan, hunkered down at the corner of the barn, it seemed much longer. Finally Old Hig called, 'I ain't real sure that you're Laurie, but I'm not sure you ain't, neither, so come on up. If you ain't who you claim you are, you're both dead.'

'I believe you,' Morgan shouted. 'If we were anybody else, we wouldn't come.'

They started up the slope, Morgan holding Laurie's hand. They climbed slowly, Laurie so tired she swayed and stumbled and would have fallen if Morgan hadn't been holding her. They reached the cabin and stepped up on the porch just as Old Hig opened the door, the lamplight falling upon them.

'Inside,' he snapped at them as he put his rifle down. 'Quick so I can shut this damned door.'

Laurie stumbled into the big room and dropped down on the homemade couch. Morgan followed, Old Hig slamming and barring the door the moment he went through it. Then the old man turned and looked at them.

'I knowed it was you soon as you started up the hill, Laurie,' Old Hig said, 'but I wasn't sure about Dillard. How'd you two get hooked up?'

The old man leaned against the door, his sharp little eyes whipping from Morgan to Laurie and back to Morgan. He looked even thinner and more frail than he had the last time Morgan had seen him. He moved to a chair and sat down, walking hunched forward, his right hand pressed against his belly.

'What's the matter?' Laurie asked. 'Did

you get hurt?'

'I sure as hell did,' the old man grumbled. 'A posse stopped here and said some of your bunch from the Dry Fork held up the bank. They figgered I knowed something about it, so when I said I didn't, that bastard of a Zach Grant hit me in the belly and knocked me down, then he kicked me in the ribs. I can't breathe real good since then.'

'Probably broke some ribs,' Morgan said. 'I knew they're a poor outfit, but I didn't think Nolan would stand for anything like that.'

'I reckon that booger would have killed me,' Old Hig said, 'but Craig stopped him. Nolan didn't lift a finger.' He studied Laurie a moment, then added, 'Girl, you sure look like you was sent for and couldn't come. You never got around to tellin' me how you two got hooked up. Don't look right, you cavortin' around this time o' night with a young buck like Dillard.'

'I feel like I'd been sent for and couldn't come,' she said. 'I've found out one thing. I'm not as stout as I thought I was. I'm tired.'

'I asked you...' Old Hig began.

'I'll tell you,' Morgan broke in. 'Laurie's got to have a place where she can sleep. We couldn't think of any place that's safer than here.' He nodded at Laurie. 'If I leave anything out, stop me and put it in.'

He told Old Hig about the robbery and Laurie taking the money and hiding it and coming to him. He said he'd taken her to the Albert ranch and explained why they'd left. He paused, looking at the old man's thin, bony face, and wondered if Higgins had been seriously injured when he'd been beaten. It could be enough to kill a man as old as he was.

'We were hoping you would let her stay with you,' Morgan said. 'Have you got a place where you can hide her?'

Old Hig didn't answer the question. He leaned forward, his hand still clutching his belly. 'I've got a rat's nest,' he muttered. 'Ain't no fit place for a decent girl.' He looked at Laurie as if trying to make up his mind about letting her stay, then he asked, 'Dillard leave out anything?'

'I guess you know what's happened to Dry Fork valley,' Laurie said, 'and how Kirk Lamm and his partners stole our water.'

'Sure I know about it,' Old Hig said impatiently. 'Likewise I know your pa's flat broke and he's a fool for staying.'

'That's why I thought of robbing the bank,' Laurie said. 'Seemed like it was wrong for my folks to starve to death after having such a good ranch. It would be different if Lamm and his company had any right to the water.'

'Sure it would,' the old man agreed. 'I

124

reckon if I was Lee Jameson, I'd have killed me a banker before now, but Lee ain't built like I am.'

'Or me,' Laurie said. 'Only I never intended to really steal the money. I thought we would make a deal with them, you know, trade the money for the water, but I found out Pony and Banjo and Doak intended to keep the money. That's why I hid it after I left the camp, then I took your mare and rode down the mountain to Peace Creek.'

Old Hig cackled. 'I knowed somebody took her. That's all I could tell that infernal posse.' He nodded at Morgan. 'Dillard, you ain't got nothing to do with the Dry Fork folks. How come you bought into this ruckus?'

'I owe Lee Jameson something,' Morgan said, 'and I owe Kirk Lamm something a whole lot different. Looks like he'll have my ranch, come fall.'

'I see,' Old Hig said thoughtfully. 'Well sir, I guess there ain't a man in the country who don't owe Kirk Lamm and his bunch of high binders something.'

'Laurie ain't told me where she hid the money,' Morgan said. 'If she don't tell you, you can't tell nobody else.'

'I don't want to know,' Old Hig said quickly. 'I dunno, girl, 'bout you stayin' here. Bartlett and his boys will tear Dillard's place up tryin' to find that dinero. If they don't, they'll come here, figurin' you might have hid it with me. They can get right down persuasive, too. Pony's a tough hombre when he sets his mind to it.'

'And the posse will be back if they don't run Bartlett and the boys down,' Morgan added. 'They might be here anyhow since they won't find the money on Pony. Both outfits will be riding through these hills hunting and shooting each other, and you're likely to get caught in the squeeze. I know Laurie can get into trouble if she stays here, but I likewise know she's sure to be in trouble if she rides with me.'

'Yeah,' Old Hig admitted. 'You and her both if they catch her with you.'

'I asked you once if you could hide her.'

'I heard you,' the old man snapped irritably. 'I can hide her, all right. I just wasn't sure whether I should.' He pointed to a bear rug on the floor. 'I've got a hole yonder she can hide in. Nobody but me knows about it. I dug it and put in a trap door when I built the cabin 'cause the Injuns was roamin' around here then and I didn't get along with some o' the chiefs.' He shook his head. 'It's a hell of a place for you to hide, girl.'

'I don't mind,' she said.

Old Hig turned to Morgan. 'What are you fixing to do while she hides? The posse's huntin' Bartlett and the boys, and both

126

bunches are huntin' Laurie. Maybe you oughtta hide, too.'

'No,' Morgan said. 'I'm going to build me a big fire and wait. Maybe the posse will show up to see who it is. If it does, I'll try to wangle a talk with Nolan. I'll see if I can make a deal with him for Laurie.'

'Yeah, you'll see some of 'em,' Old Hig said, 'and then you might wind up in the Harmony calaboose. It's worth tryin', though.' He jerked a thumb to the west. 'You'll find a good spot not far from here. Just below the Point.'

'I know the place.' Morgan rose. 'Time I got along. Put Laurie to bed.'

The girl had gone to sleep on the couch, her head tipped forward. Old Hig rose. 'I'll straighten her out and cover her up right here. I don't figger on sleeping till daylight.'

'Take care of her,' Morgan said and, lifting the bar, opened the door and stepped outside.

He walked rapidly down the slope to the barn, led his horse outside, tightened the cinch, and mounted. He followed the road until he was opposite the place Old Hig had mentioned, a clearing directly below a jutting pinnacle of rock called the Point.

Morgan turned, north, and when he reached the clearing, he rode across it to the far end, dismounted, and built a fire. He stripped gear from the sorrel and tied him in the quaking asps so he could not be seen by anyone entering the clearing, then he sat down beside the fire to wait.

CHAPTER FOURTEEN

The air steadily turned colder through the early morning hours. Morgan fell asleep several times, but the fire burned down and the cold always woke him. He threw more wood on the fire and hunkered beside it again, his coat collar turned up, his saddle blanket wrapped around his shoulders.

Slowly the night-black sky above the eastern ridge began to grow lighter and the stars began to fade. The cloak of darkness that had hidden the opposite side of the clearing from Morgan gave way to opalescent dawn, and the walls of quaking asps that surrounded the little park took shape, their white trunks ghostly in the half light. A thin mist rose from the ground, giving a strange and weird appearance to the entire clearing.

Morgan had almost given up hope that his plan was going to work, then he heard horses coming toward him. He built up the fire and moved back into the timber, leaving his saddle and blanket beside the fire. He squatted in the vague fringe of the firelight and, drawing his revolver, laid it on the ground between his feet.

The horses apparently stopped for a time, then Morgan heard them again. Presently two riders appeared in the south end of the clearing. They stopped again, one of the men calling, 'Who is it?'

'Dillard,' Morgan answered. 'Who are you?'

'Craig,' the man said. 'Lamm's with me. You alone?'

'I'm alone,' Morgan said. 'Come on in.'

They rode toward him, slowly as if reluctant to come too close. When they were halfway across the clearing, Craig asked, 'What in hell are you doing here, Dillard? You've built a fire so big you can't get close to it. We saw it a mile away. Why ain't you home?'

'I've got business with Nolan,' Morgan answered. 'Where is he?'

'Right behind you,' Nolan said. 'Don't make any fast moves, Dillard. I've got my gun in my hand and it's lined on your backbone right between your shoulder blades.'

Morgan sighed. 'Where's your horse?'

'In the other side of the clearing,' Nolan said. 'Craig and Lamm waited until I circled so I could come in behind you. He couldn't see who you were. We figured you were Pony Bartlett.'

'Pony's got a little sense,' Morgan said. 'He wouldn't build a fire like this to bring you to him.'

'He might if he wanted to make a deal,' Nolan said. 'Now what business have you got with me? Nobody in Harmony hooked you up with the robbery, so unless you know where they are, you'd better be damned quick with this business of yours.'

Craig and Lamm had ridden up to the fire and sat their saddles staring at Morgan. Craig said, 'I'll go fetch your horse, Frank.'

'Go ahead,' Nolan said. 'I don't figure to be here long. Get on your feet, Dillard, and turn around.'

'No,' Morgan said. 'I don't trust you worth a damn. You come around and stand in front of me.'

'I don't trust you, neither,' Nolan said.

Morgan's right hand had dropped to the ground between his legs. Now it closed over the butt of his gun. He said, 'You listen, Nolan. I've got a deal to offer you, but I ain't talking to a man who's got his gun lined on my backbone. I'm here to do you a favor. You're as big a crook as Lamm. You're partners with him in the company that stole the water from the Dry Fork ranchers. The way I see it, stealing money from a bank is no worse than stealing water from ranchers who've got to have it making a living.'

'I suppose shooting my boy is no worse,

either,' Lamm broke in hoarsely. 'Maybe you're God, Dillard, telling us one crime is no worse than another.'

'If I was God, I'd know what to do with you,' Morgan flung at him. 'But not being God, I can still say it's no worse to shoot a man than it is to starve him to death, or let him die because he can't get a doctor. You drove Pony Bartlett to robbing your bank and now you're hunting him.'

'You know where he is?' Nolan demanded.

'Come around in front of me if we're going to talk.' Morgan saw Lamm's hand drop to his gun butt, and he said sharply, 'Don't touch your iron, Lamm. I didn't build this fire and freeze to death to fetch you here to shoot you, but I don't aim to be shot, neither.'

Lamm's hand moved to his saddle horn. He was tired and dirty, his black broadcloth suit was soiled, his face was stubble-covered, and he had the whipped look of a man who had been toppled off his throne. Now he bowed his head, his gaze on his hands that were cupped around the saddle horn.

They were this way, all three of them motionless until Orlando Craig returned leading Nolan's horse. He looked at them, then he said, 'When I was a kid in school, we used to play a game called "statue." You boys playing it?'

'I guess we are,' Morgan said. 'I told Nolan I came here to do him a favor, but I won't talk to a man who's standing behind me with a gun in my back.'

'Hell's bells, Frank,' Craig said in disgust. 'Come here. I don't blame Dillard. Let's hear what he's got to say and ride out.' Nolan still hesitated, then Craig shouted, 'Damn it, Frank, sometimes you act like a two-year-old. I know Dillard. He didn't have any part in the robbery, and he won't pick up his iron and shoot all three of us.'

Nolan grunted something, then moved into the clearing, his gun still in his hand. He said, 'All right, Dillard. Make it quick.'

'Put your gun into your holster,' Morgan ordered.

Again Nolan hesitated, glaring at Morgan, and again Craig shouted, 'I'm clean out of patience, Frank. Do what he tells you and get on your horse.'

Nolan wheeled to face the storekeeper. 'You've lost all the sense you ever had, Orlando. Maybe I'll want to take Dillard to jail. Why should I deal him all the trumps?'

'If you point that gun at me, I'll kill you,' Morgan said. 'I ain't going to be locked up in your jail. I've told you and I'll tell you once more. I'm here to do you a favor. If you don't want it, get on your horse and ride out of here, but you'll never put me into your stinking calaboose.'

132

Nolan cursed and jammed his gun into leather. 'Let's hear your favor.'

'I don't know where your money is,' Morgan said, 'but I can get it if you're willing to trade. If you don't get the money back into your bank, the bank's broke. The way it stands, Lee Jameson and everybody else who's still hanging on in Dry Fork valley is broke, so why not make a swap, the money for the water?'

Lamm looked up 'We'll do it,' he said eagerly. 'To hell with the irrigation scheme. We're all ruined if the bank goes. You know that as well as I do, Nolan.'

The sheriff grinned. 'You're forgetting something, Kirk. You're not running the show. I am. I say no deal.' He turned to Morgan. 'Now just how would you find the money, Dillard?'

'My business,' Morgan said. 'I made my offer, but you turned it down, so the talk's over.'

Nolan moistened his lips with the tip of his tongue and glanced at Craig. 'Well, Orlando, what do you think of that? This bastard didn't have no part in the robbery, you said. Well, if he didn't, how does he know about the money?'

'You get the Jameson girl and you've got the answer to your question,' Craig said. 'Come on, let's see if we can pick up the trail of the men we're after. If the girl's got the money, and it sure looks that way, you can bet your bottom dollar that Bartlett and his two pals are around here looking for her. They're not going to hide out in the lava beds without that dinero.'

'Smart thinking, Orlando,' Nolan conceded. 'Is he right, Dillard?'

'I've had my say,' Morgan said. 'Mount up, Sheriff. I'm staying right here till you're on the other side of the clearing, then I'm riding. Don't come after me because I won't be taken. I haven't committed any crime, but I'm afraid of what would happen if you got me into your jail.'

'You've got a right to be afraid of what would happen,' Craig said. 'Come on, Kirk.'

Craig and Lamm turned their horses and rode across the clearing. For a moment Nolan stood motionless, his hands fisted, his face dark with the fury that churned through him, then he said, 'You'll see my jail, bucko. Don't you ever doubt it. You were in that bank robbery up to your neck, and before I'm done, I'll prove it.'

He turned to his horse, mounted, and rode after the other two. Quickly Morgan saddled his sorrel, jammed his Winchester into the boot, and rode up the slope toward the summit. He didn't know what he would do or where he would go. All he wanted to do now was to stay out of Nolan's reach.

CHAPTER FIFTEEN

Frank Nolan was so angry when he rode across the clearing that he couldn't think coherently. Orlando Craig had been the one who had spotted the campfire and had insisted on checking it out. Nolan had not expected to find the men they were after, but he had agreed to look into it to satisfy Craig, so he had carefully circled the clearing on foot, expecting to surprise the man at the fire.

Nolan was sore when he saw that the man was Dillard who had no business being here; he was even more angry when Dillard with Craig's help succeeded in maneuvering him around in front with his gun in his holster. He had a short moment of triumph when he turned Dillard's offer down, but knew at once he had made a mistake.

Lamm was right. Keeping the bank solvent was more important than developing the irrigation project. Knowing this simply added to his rage. But for Craig to ride off and take Lamm with him, leaving Nolan with no choice except to follow, was too much.

By the time he reached the quaking asps at the south end of the clearing, Nolan had made up his mind to turn around and go after Dillard. He didn't actually believe it when he'd told Dillard he was into the robbery up to his neck, but the man had got the best of him. He probably knew where the money was, or, as Craig had suggested, the Jameson girl knew, and the chances were Dillard could lead him to the girl.

Nolan started to rein his horse around when he saw Simon Pratt riding toward him from the road. The blacksmith waved his hand and yelled something. Lamm spurred his horse into a run, obviously excited. Pratt wheeled his mount and started back toward the road.

Craig turned in his saddle to call, 'Come on, Frank. They've jumped our men.' The storekeeper put his horse into a run to catch up with Lamm and Pratt.

For a moment Nolan hesitated, caught between his anger and hurt pride and the compulsion to get even with Dillard on one hand and the obvious course of duty on the other. He had been a lawman for a long time; his habits as a lawman were formed so firmly that he had no choice. He dug in the steel and caught up with Lamm and Craig by the time they reached the road.

Grant and Clint Jones were out of sight, but Pratt was visible ahead of them as he threaded his way through the quaking asps. Nolan knew this country south of the road and west of the divide, cut by a maze of canyons so that if Grant and Jones didn't catch up with the bank robbers in a few minutes, they probably wouldn't catch them at all. There were simply too many ways they could go, too many places to hide.

If Grant and Jones lost sight of the fugitives and Grant had to track them, they would be miles away by dark. A few minutes later Nolan and the two men with him broke out of the quaking asps and found themselves in open country with only a few scattered spruce trees.

They gained steadily on Pratt, catching him just before he dropped down a sharp pitch into a narrow canyon that was heavily timbered. A thick growth of willows made a jungle on the banks of the small stream in the bottom.

'You sure you're on Grant's tail?' Nolan demanded.

Pratt shot him an irritated glance. 'Of course I'm sure. I seen 'em all the time till 'bout five minutes ago when they hit this timber.'

When they reached the stream, Nolan was surprised to find Grant standing beside his heaving horse. Jones was still in the saddle, his gaze on Grant who apparently had been examining the tracks in the damp dirt beside the creek.

'I can't figure this, Frank,' Grant said. 'They split just above here. We lost sight of 'em when they hit the timber. They were lucky to run onto a game trail, so they moved faster'n we did. By the time Clint'n me got to the creek, they was out of sight, but I seen fresh tracks of one horse going down. I worked upstream a piece and found where they separated. Two of 'em had struck off up the creek.'

'What is there about this you don't figure?' Nolan demanded.

'Why they split,' Grant said. 'Looks like three of 'em fighting together would make it tougher on us than it will be now.'

Nolan guessed that Pony Bartlett was the rider who had gone downstream and the two boys had gone the other way. If Dillard had been telling the truth and if Craig's guess about the Jameson girl was right, Bartlett and the boys did not have the money. Rather than strike out for the lava beds which was the natural hideout, they had returned to the Catclaws to find the girl and the money.

'How'd you happen to spot them in the first place?' Nolan asked.

'We was breaking camp,' Grant said, 'figuring you'd be back any time and tell us what to do. Clint here seen somebody on the road riding by like they owned the mountains. I guess they didn't figure we were anywhere around. As soon as I seen there was three of 'em, I lit a shuck for the road. I recognized Pony Bartlett when I got a

138

little closer to 'em, so I told Simon to get the rest of you, then me'n Clint took after 'em. Soon as they seen we was on their tail, they took off into the quakies.'

'Which way were they headed?' Nolan asked. 'Up or down?'

'Up,' Grant answered.

'What the hell are we standing around here for?' Lamm demanded. 'They're getting farther away all the time.'

'If you're so damned smart,' Nolan snapped, 'maybe you'd like to tell us what to do?'

'I sure would,' Lamm said hotly. 'We ought to go after both of 'em. I'll take two men and go up the creek. The other three of you go downstream. If we keep the pressure on them, we'll catch up with them.'

'All right,' Nolan said. 'You've been trying to call the turn ever since we started, so you can take two men and get yourself killed. I'm tired of listening to you. Which two do you want?'

'Grant and Pratt,' Lamm answered.

Nolan nodded. 'All right. Orlando and Clint goes with me. Come on.'

Nolan wheeled his horse downstream, watching the tracks beside the creek. He doubted that his man would stay in the bottom of the canyon unless he planned to ambush them. Nolan glanced back once to see that Craig and Jones were following him.

139

The other three had already disappeared.

Presently the canyon walls slanted back so they were not as steep as they had been farther up, the timber was more scattered, and the valley was almost level, the stream meandering through a dense thicket of willows that was taller than a man's head. Nolan reined up until Craig and Jones reached him. The tracks still followed the stream. The outlaw had made no effort to hide them, so it seemed evident to Nolan that the man wanted the posse to track him.

'What are we stopping for?' Craig demanded, pointing to the tracks in the mud. 'We're getting close.'

'Too close,' Nolan said. 'You know Pony Bartlett pretty well, Orlando?'

Craig scratched the back of his neck, glancing at Jones and then at Nolan. 'Yeah, I used to. Why?'

'I've got a hunch it's Bartlett we're following. He's baited a trap for us.' Nolan jerked a thumb downstream. 'He's lying down there in them willows just waiting for us to ride up close enough so he can't miss. Before we ever saw him, we'd all three be lying in the dirt.'

'You mean you're turning around because we caught up with him?' Craig demanded.

'Well, we don't want to get dry gulched, do we?' Nolan asked. 'Besides, Lamm is going to need us before long. That's a dead end canyon he's riding up.'

'You let him—' Craig demanded.

'I didn't let him,' Nolan said harshly. 'You heard him. I'm getting tired of him sulking because he's not running this shebang. I figured he'd better run some of it awhile. Likewise I'm tired of you sticking your nose into the posse's business, like siding with Morgan Dillard while ago.'

Craig flushed. 'I've kept you from making a few mistakes. That's all.'

'Then keep me from making another one,' Nolan said. 'Like riding into those willows and getting the top of my head blowed off. Besides, you claim the Jameson girl has the money and we've got to find it to keep the bank from going broke.'

'What's that got to do with going after Bartlett?' Craig asked. 'He don't know where she is.'

'No, but as long as she's got the money, Bartlett's not going to leave the Catclaws, so we can pick him up later. If your guess about the girl is right, and I think it is, we'd better find her. We'll start looking at Old Hig's place. We know she wasn't in Dillard's cabin last night because we looked, and it's not likely she went back to it. The Alberts claim she left the valley. Well, we likewise know she wasn't with Dillard this morning. She's sure not going to be riding through these mountains alone. The way I see it, that leaves Old Hig's place.'

'I don't know,' Craig said doubtfully. 'She knows we'd look for her there. I...'

He stopped, his head tipped to one side. Nolan heard it then, the sharp crackle of rifle fire from far up the canyon. 'I guess we'd better go give our banker hand,' Nolan said. 'Sounds like he walked into it.'

Nolan turned his horse and rode back the way they had come. Craig and Jones exchanged glances, then fell in behind him. They thought he didn't have guts enough to go in after Bartlett, he told himself. Well, let them think what they damn please. Right now he didn't care anything about Pony Bartlett. Or Kirk Lamm.

The only person he wanted was the Jameson girl. If he found her and if she knew where the money was, he'd get it out of her. This time Orlando Craig wouldn't stop him. He'd take care of Pony Bartlett and Morgan Dillard later.

CHAPTER SIXTEEN

Kirk Lamm's world broke up the moment his son Bud was murdered and the bank robbed. He had been forced to join the posse, his advice had been ignored, he had been physically beaten, he had been

142

humiliated repeatedly by Nolan, and he was sore and stiff from so much riding. He was tired and hungry and dirty. He was no better than a blacksmith like Simon Pratt, or a foul-smelling hunter and guide and odd-job man like Zach Grant.

Lamm had had no idea how much Frank Nolan hated him, but he knew now. Well, he hated the sheriff as much as the sheriff hated him. At this moment Kirk Lamm hated everybody. He hated all the members of the posse; he hated Pony Bartlett and the two boys who had murdered his son, and he hated the people who lived on the Dry Fork and had used this means of striking back at him.

Most of all Lamm hated himself. Just a few hours ago he had been the most powerful man in Harmony, the richest man in the county, the banker who held the future of everyone else on Smoky river in the palm of his hand. It had never occurred to him that he might be toppled from his throne, but that was exactly what had happened.

Lamm had not been strong enough to hold the position he had attained. That was why he had to regain his confidence and his strength. Once he had done that, he could face Frank Nolan and kill him if that became necessary.

Now, riding up the narrow canyon as hard as he could, he began to feel confident and strong. He didn't know which two of the three bank robbers they were pursuing. It didn't make any difference. They were all responsible for Bud's murder. He'd capture them and kill them. It wouldn't be murder. It would be an execution. He wouldn't let them be taken back to Harmony to be put into jail. There was too much chance they would be acquitted by a jury ...

He heard the snap of a bullet inches from the side of his head; he heard the solid *thwack* of a slug as it hit Simon Pratt who was riding a little ways behind him, and he heard the sharp crack of rifles. He was aware that Pratt threw up his hands and rolled out of his saddle, hitting the ground like a sack of wool; he was aware that Grant yelled, 'Get under cover, Lamm.'

He reined sharply to his left and brought his horse to a stop behind a tall boulder just as the rifles cracked again, one of the bullets glancing off the big rock beside his head. He heard it scream as it ricocheted across the canyon; he felt the sting of rock particles striking the side of his face. He dismounted and, raising a hand to his cheek, brought it in front of his eyes and stared at it stupidly. His fingers were covered with blood.

In that moment his new feeling of strength and confidence fled from him. He saw himself for what he was, a weak man who had hidden from the world behind a façade of power and position. When that façade was tumbled to the ground, he was exposed as a naked, trembling man to anyone who looked at him.

Zach Grant had pulled in behind another boulder just below Lamm. Now he darted around it to stand beside Lamm, leaving his horse ground-hitched. He saw the blood and asked, 'You hit?'

Lamm shook his head. 'Just scratched up by some rock splinters.'

'We got careless,' Grant said. 'I forgot this was a dead end canyon. We've got our men cornered because they couldn't run any farther, but damned if I know what to do with 'em.' He jerked a thumb at Pratt who hadn't moved after he hit the ground. 'Looks like Simon's done for.'

Lamm hadn't looked at the blacksmith. He hadn't even thought about the man. He closed his hands into fists and shut his eyes. All he wanted to do was to keep himself from screaming or running or getting on his horse and riding back down the canyon like the coward that he knew he was. When he opened his eyes, he saw that Grant was studying the steep north wall of the canyon.

'We were riding hell for leather,' Grant was saying, 'figuring our men was trying to get away, but if I'd looked ahead at that rimrock, I could of seen we'd get to the end. Now they're up yonder and it's a standoff. If we even try to get a drink from the creek, they'll put a window in our skulls pronto.'

Grant kept on studying the north wall. Lamm asked 'You've got an idea of some kind, haven't you?'

'Why yes, you might say I have,' Grant said. 'I've got an idea I'd like to get out of this damned cold country and go to Arizona, but I never made enough money to get off Smoky river or out of the Catclaws. Maybe I will now. If I get these two boys for you, does that mean I'll have one-half of the reward money? We're after four of 'em, and two's half of four the way I figure.'

'Sure you'd get half,' Lamm said eagerly, 'but we're pinned down. I don't see how...'

'Mister Banker,' Grant said, 'all you've got to do is to poke your noggin around this here rock you're hiding behind and shoot once in a while. I figure our two bank robbers will come walking down the canyon in less'n ten minutes. Now start shooting.'

Lamm drew his Winchester from the boot, jacked a shell into the chamber, and moved to the edge of the boulder. He threw a shot in the general direction of the upper end of the canyon and jerked back. He immediately drew two answering shots.

'Good,' Grant said. 'Now let go on this side so they'll think we're both in the game.'

Lamm obeyed and again drew two shots, the bullets kicking up dust downstream from

146

the boulder. Grant nodded. 'Now from that side. Repeat it just like this every few minutes. If you forget, they might spot me. If they knock me off the side of the canyon, you'll be in a hell of a tight spot.'

Again Lamm obeyed. When he jerked back to safety, he saw that Grant had started to work his way up the north wall. At first glance Lamm didn't understand why the fugitives didn't shoot Grant, then he discovered what the man must have seen before he started, a zig-zag row of boulders nested on the cliff in such a way as to give him cover halfway or more to the rim.

The boulders had dropped from the top of the canyon wall two hundred feet or more above the bottom. Several, including the one in front of Lamm, had rolled all the way down, but the others had lodged on the cliff.

Watching Grant edge his way up the canyon wall, Lamm had the feeling the man was gambling with his life, that it would take very little to bring a rock slide thundering down on top of him. Suddenly he remembered what he was supposed to be doing. He fired from one side of the boulder, and then from the other, and looked up again. Grant had stopped, apparently having gone high enough to have the drop on the bank robbers.

'Freeze,' Grant yelled. 'I can drill both of you. If you try to run that's what I'll do. Now

147

get on your feet and drop your gun belts, then hook the moon.'

'You go to hell,' one of the fugitives shouted defiantly. 'If you think...'

Grant fired. Before the echoes of his shot died, he said, 'From where I am, I can shoot the wings off a fly that's on one of your noses. Now get off that rock and start walking. One wrong move from either one of you and you're dead.'

Apparently Grant's shot convinced them. A moment later he called, 'Here they come, Lamm. Cover 'em and keep 'em covered. I'll be with you in a minute.'

Lamm stepped to the side of the big rock, his Winchester held on the ready. The two bank robbers were walking toward him, their hands in the air. He recognized them, Banjo Smith and Doak Watts, boys who were very little older than his son they had murdered. For a moment his finger tightened on the trigger and he had to fight a compulsion to shoot both of them.

'Where's the money you stole from the bank?' Lamm demanded.

'We don't know,' Banjo Smith answered. 'If we had it, we wouldn't be here.'

Lamm watched them come toward him, both of them scared. They had a right to be, he told himself. He had no intention of letting them leave the canyon alive. Then he remembered the big spruce tree a short distance downstream and he knew what he was going to do.

He stepped aside for them to pass, the corners of his mouth working as hate burned through him. Both looked at him as they came opposite. He said, 'Keep going.'

He fell in behind them and followed until they reached the spruce. He said, 'Stop.'

They obeyed. Banjo Smith glanced over his shoulder at Lamm, asking, 'What are you fixing to do?'

He didn't answer. Doak Watts said, 'Don't beg the bastard. He's going to kill us just like he killed Pony Bartlett's wife and baby.'

Lamm wanted to cry out that they were wrong, that he had nothing to do with the death of Mrs Bartlett and her baby, but he didn't. He remained silent until Grant reached him. He said, 'Fetch their horses.'

'What do you aim to...,' Grant began.

'Damn it, do what I tell you,' Lamm screamed.

Spit drooled down his chin. He swallowed and wiped a sleeve across his mouth, his body tense, his gaze on the backs of the boys in front of him. Grant stared at him, then he shrugged and walked up the creek. He returned in a few minutes with the horses.

'Tie their hands behind their backs,' Lamm ordered.

Grant obeyed. Lamm said, 'Put the ropes

around their necks and throw the ends over that limb above them. Then get them into their saddles.'

'Now hold on,' Grant said. 'It ain't our business...'

'Damn it,' Lamm yelled, 'do what I tell you and quit arguing or you'll never see Arizona.'

Again Grant obeyed and Lamm nodded. 'All right, tie the ends to that other tree.'

'I ain't sure this is gonna break their necks,' Grant said. 'Might just strangle 'em. We sure don't have no proper hangman's knot.'

'They're dead either way, aren't they?' Lamm demanded.

Doak Watts had been silent, but Banjo Smith had been cursing Lamm. Now he said, 'Lamm, you son of a bitch, we'll beat you getting to hell, and when you walk in, we're going to black-ball you so even the devil won't have you.'

Lamm said nothing. When the ropes had been tied to the tree, he took off his hat and hit one of the horses on the rump and then the other, yelling at them. They lunged forward, the boys were yanked out of their saddles and dropped. Banjo's neck apparently was broken, but Grant decided that Doak's wasn't. Drawing his gun, Grant shot him in the chest.

Grant stared at the boys for a moment,

then suddenly he was sick. He walked away, retching. Later he came back and said, 'You're a mean bastard, Lamm. I hope you get what's coming to you.'

Lamm didn't even look at Grant. He stood with his head tipped back, his gaze on the swaying bodies, and felt a strange, satisfying sweetness wash through him.

CHAPTER SEVENTEEN

When Morgan Dillard rode out of the clearing early that morning, he had every expectation that Frank Nolan would follow him. He had not really expected them to accept the deal he had offered, but he'd had to try for Laurie's sake. What had surprised him the most was Orlando Craig's support. He sensed the hostility that lay between Nolan and Craig, and he saw, too, that Kirk Lamm was only a shell of a man who was totally unlike the hard, tight-fisted banker Morgan had talked to in Harmony only a short time before.

Well, you found out a lot about people that you didn't know when they faced a crisis, Morgan told himself as he rode upslope. Knowing Laurie as a girl, he had never thought she would take part in a bank robbery. Knowing Pony Bartlett as a man, he was not surprised that he would hold up a bank, but he was surprised that Bartlett would break his word with Laurie about keeping the stolen money.

Reaching a tall upthrust of sandstone, Morgan pulled in behind it and dismounted. He drew his Winchester from the boot and climbed to the top of the rock and lay flat on his belly, his gaze sweeping the quaking asps and scrub oak below him, but there was no hint of movement. Nolan hadn't followed him after all.

Morgan remained there a long time, the sun lifting into a clear sky and cutting away the night chill. He thought about Nolan. He had known the sheriff as a tough, proud man, one who would not overlook the fact that he had been humiliated this morning. Sooner or later Morgan would have to face him and have it out with him, and that, he told himself sourly, might make an outlaw out of him. If he ran into Pony Bartlett, he'd do well to join up with him.

He slid off the rock, jammed his rifle into the scabbard, and mounted. He rode warily, not wanting to run into the posse, but fully aware that it was a possibility. He wasn't sure how it would go if he did, but the chances were Nolan would try to take him.

If that happened, Morgan would kill somebody. He asked himself how he'd ever got into a deadly game like this, but when he thought about the events of the last twenty-four hours beginning with finding Laurie in the haystack, he had no regrets.

He angled upslope for a time, then cut directly south because he didn't want to get too close to Old Hig's cabin in case he did run into the posse. He reined up occasionally and listened, but it was not until he had crossed the road that he heard shots from the upper end of the canyon ahead of him.

At first he told himself it was not his fight and he'd do well to ride back the way he had come. Curiosity as much as anything drew him on south to the rim. The only reason he was riding at all was to be close enough to Old Hig's cabin to help out if either the posse or the bank robbers got the idea of looking there for Laurie.

Another idea had been working in his mind. If Laurie was cooped up in Old Hig's cabin for any length of time, she wouldn't have a chance to make a deal for the water, so it seemed to Morgan it was still up to him to do it for her. The fact that Nolan had turned him down didn't mean anything. Craig and Lamm would have taken the offer if Nolan had let them. There were other men in Harmony who would be interested, men like Doc Vance. They were the men Morgan wanted to see.

By the time he came to the canyon, he had made up his mind that Laurie would be safe until dark and he'd have time to go into Harmony and get back. When he reached the rim and saw Kirk Lamm slap his hat across the rumps of the horses that held Banjo Smith and Doak Watts, Morgan forgot about going to town.

The hanging was over within a matter of seconds from the time Morgan reached the rim. Even if he had arrived sooner, he was too far away to have saved the boys' lives. He sat his saddle, horrified and shocked and thinking that what he was looking at was so incredible it must be a nightmare.

Any way you looked at it, Kirk Lamm and Zach Grant had committed murder. If Frank Nolan was any kind of a proper sheriff, he'd take Lamm and Grant to jail when he found out what had happened.

But Nolan didn't do any such thing when he rode up a few minutes later with Orlando Craig and Clint Jones. Morgan couldn't hear what was being said, but he had a hunch Craig was calling it murder.

In any case, the argument between Craig and Nolan was short and fierce. From where Morgan sat his saddle, it looked as if it might turn into a fight, but suddenly Craig wheeled his horse and said something to Clint Jones. They picked up Simon Pratt's body, tied it face down across his saddle, and rode away.

Craig and Jones were leaving the posse. That seemed plain enough. Only three men were left. In a way that was a good thing. It made better odds if Nolan decided to move in on Old Hig and Morgan was pulled into the fight. On the other hand, it was bad in the sense that Orlando Craig was the one man in the bunch who used his head and held to some standard of human decency. Frank Nolan hadn't, or he wouldn't overlook the hanging.

Craig and Jones must be heading back to town. When that thought struck Morgan, he made up his mind. He'd take the bodies into town and he'd get Craig and Doc Vance and anyone else he could to sign an agreement to run water back into the Dry Fork canal in exchange for the stolen money. The way things were developing, he had a feeling that Frank Nolan and Kirk Lamm were finished on Smoky river.

Morgan waited until Nolan, Lamm and Grant rode downstream. When they were out of sight, Morgan followed the rim until he found a place where he could work his way to the bottom. He found the boys' horses and led them back up the creek to where the bodies still swung in the wind from the limb of the spruce tree. He cut them down, tied them in the saddles, and led the horses out of the canyon.

By the time Morgan reached Harmony, it was well after noon. He stopped in front of Doc Vance's office, but the medico was gone. Morgan carried the bodies inside and laid them on tables in Vance's back room, put the horses in the livery stable, and had dinner in a restaurant.

'You know where Doc is?' Morgan asked as he paid for his meal.

'Yeah, he drove out to Poverty Flat,' the man said. 'Seems like Lee Jameson got beat up pretty bad when the posse was out there trying to find the bank robbers. Missus Jameson came in this morning to get Doc. He didn't want to go, knowing he wouldn't get paid, but Missus Jameson finally talked him into it.'

Morgan went outside, thinking this was something else Frank Nolan and Zach Grant and the rest of them would have to pay for. He paused on the board walk as he saw Doc Vance pull his buggy to a stop in front of the Belle Union, tie his horse, and go in, his derby cocked at the usual jaunty angle. Better get it over with, Morgan decided, and followed Vance into the saloon.

The doctor had just taken off his sheepskin and pulled back a chair at a table where Craig and Clint Jones were sitting when Morgan pushed through the batwings. He walked directly to the table and sat down.

Craig stared at Morgan in astonishment, then demanded, 'What are you doing in town? I thought you were riding around in the Catclaws.'

'I've got a question for you,' Morgan said. 'Why ain't you with the posse? Clint, too?'

Craig looked away, red-faced. He said, 'You know?'

Morgan nodded. 'I was on the rim when Lamm dropped 'em out of their saddles.' He turned to Vance. 'How's Lee Jameson?'

'He'll be all right,' the doctor said. 'He's busted up some and won't be working for a while. Now will you tell me what you're talking about?'

'Lamm and Grant hung Banjo Smith and Doak Watts this morning,' Morgan said. 'I brought the bodies in. They're in your back room. With you being the coroner, I figured you'd want to see 'em.'

'You mean they were lynched?' Vance asked as if he didn't believe it.

'That's what I mean,' Morgan said. 'I hope I get a chance to go into court and testify that Lamm and Grant murdered them. What's the matter with Nolan? Is he going to stand for prisoners being lynched by his posse?'

Craig poured himself a drink and gulped it. Jones said, 'We asked him that. He claimed they had to go after Pony Bartlett and he wasn't going to get sidetracked. That's when Orlando and me got a bellyful of the whole business and left.' He spread his hands. 'I dunno what's happened to this country. All of a sudden it's gone to pot.'

'You know damned well what's happened,' Morgan said hotly. 'Doc and Craig do, too. It started a long time ago when you let Kirk Lamm run everything around here, and it came to a head when you stole water from Lee Jameson and Pony Bartlett and everybody else who lived on the Dry Fork. The sheriff himself was in on it. You ought to be in jail, the whole rotten bunch of you.'

'Not me,' Clint Jones said quickly. 'I didn't have nothing to do with it. All I've ever done is to run a saloon. I told the boys when they stole that water—'

'Shut up.' Craig turned to Morgan. 'Sure we ought to be in jail. I'm ashamed of letting Lee Jameson get beat up. I'm ashamed of Doc for not taking care of the folks out there on Poverty Flat and I'm ashamed of whatever part I had in Pony Bartlett's wife and baby dying and in running a lot of decent folks off their property. I'm ashamed of a lot of things, but mostly for standing by and letting Kirk Lamm do anything he wanted.'

Craig took another drink and leaned forward until his face was close to Morgan's. 'Dillard, you've bought into this business when it wasn't any real concern of yours, but maybe you can answer a question. How does a man get off a merry-go-round like this once you're on it?'

'That's what I want to know.' Vance said. 'I'm ready to get off, too.'

'I know one thing,' Craig said. 'When the posse comes in, we're going to do something. Frank Nolan's giving up his star and Kirk Lamm is going to understand he's not running things any more.'

'There's more to it than that,' Morgan said. 'You're right about one thing. I have bought into this business and I aim to see it through. Grant and Lamm are going to jail for murder.'

'All right, we'll help you,' Craig said. 'Maybe you'd like the sheriff's job?'

'No, but I'll take it if you don't find someone who's better,' Morgan said. 'Now how about getting off that merry-go-round?'

'What do you mean?' Craig asked.

'I told you this morning,' Morgan said. 'The stolen money for the water you stole.'

'We wouldn't hesitate about taking that kind of a deal,' Vance said. 'The bank's what's important. We've got to keep it solvent or we're all broke.'

Craig studied Morgan for a moment, then he asked, 'Are you sure you can deliver the money?'

'I'm sure.'

Craig nodded. 'All right, you've got a deal. It's like Doc says. The bank is what's important. You fetch the money in tonight and I'll see that a crew of men are working on the canal first thing in the morning.'

'No questions asked about who gave me the money?' Morgan asked.

'No questions,' Craig answered. 'I don't know how you're going to work this, but you may have trouble with Nolan. He's got a notion the money's hidden around Old Hig's place somewhere and he aims to make the old man talk.'

Morgan's heart skipped a beat. He should have stayed in the mountains close enough to Old Hig's cabin to help him and Laurie. He rose and looked down into the storekeeper's red, wind-burned face. He said, 'I'd better get there before he does.'

He left the saloon, got his horse from the livery stable, and rode west toward the Catclaws. It would be dark before he reached the summit, but maybe Nolan wouldn't make a move while it was still daylight. That was the best Morgan could hope for.

CHAPTER EIGHTEEN

Sheriff Frank Nolan was furious. His rage had been mounting since early morning. Up until then he had enjoyed the hunt, largely because it had given him a chance to humble Kirk Lamm. But today the whole deal had turned sour. First Morgan Dillard had

160

outmaneuvered him, then Lamm and Zach Grant had lynched the bank robbers who might have told them something about the money or the girl, or both. And finally Orlando Craig and Clint Jones had deserted the posse.

Nolan called a halt just above the willows where Pony Bartlett had taken refuge. They built a fire and cooked dinner, then Grant spent an hour walking along the creek trying to untangle the tracks. Finally he returned to where Lamm and Nolan squatted beside the fire, Nolan staring moodily at the flames.

'Looks to me like he came out of the willows after you boys turned around,' Grant said. 'He kept his horse in the creek a ways just to put you off the tracks, I reckon, then he took up the side of the canyon. I'd say he's up on the rim yonder just waiting for us.'

'Naw,' Nolan said. 'Getting away was all he was interested in. I'm not so sure about Dillard. If he knows where the girl and the money are, and I figure he does or he wouldn't have tried to make a swap with us this morning, then the chances are he's hiding around here somewhere waiting to dry gulch us.'

'No,' Lamm said. 'He could have done that this morning if he'd wanted to. It's Bartlett we've got to find.'

Nolan's face turned red. He felt his blood

161

pound in his ears as he fought his temper. When he had it under control, he said, 'Kirk, I thought I had you convinced it was smarter for you to take orders than to start giving them again. You forget that?'

'That's right, I forgot.' Lamm stood with his big head thrust forward, his eyes meeting Nolan's. 'I got two of my boy's murderers and I aim to get the third one. It's the bank robbers we're after, not Morgan Dillard, and don't you forget it.'

Nolan saw that Lamm had dredged up enough courage to knock heads with him. He was so surprised that he hesitated for a moment, thinking he might have to whip the banker to keep him in line, then decided it wasn't important enough now. It could wait.

'Kirk, you made a damn fool mistake hanging those boys,' Nolan said. 'Craig and Jones are going to cause us trouble. I don't know how I can keep you and Zach from hanging.'

Lamm's mouth curled in derision. 'You'll find a way, Frank. We need you and you need us. Besides, they were murderers and they would have been hung if we'd taken them back to town. Zach and I were executioners. That's all.'

'You'll have a hard time proving that in court, and unless I'm mistaken, that's where Craig is going to take it.' Nolan turned to his horse and mounted. 'Come on. We'll ride to

162

the rim and see if Zach can pick up Bartlett's trail. If he can, we'll stay on it till dark, then we're going to Old Hig's place and find out if the girl's there.'

'Even if she ain't there, the money probably is,' Grant said. 'If she's on the run, I don't think she'd be packing it with her.'

'That may be right,' Nolan conceded, 'but even if she did hide the money somewhere around Old Hig's place, he might not know.'

'I'll make him tell us,' Grant said, and turned his horse up the north wall of the canyon.

Nolan glanced at the sun, noting that it was dropping toward the western horizon. He guessed they had three or four hours of daylight left. They'd better spend it hunting Bartlett than to tackle Old Hig's place in the daytime. They'd wait till dark to do that. After the beating Old Hig had taken, he'd smoke them down the instant he saw them.

Nolan was thinking about it as they climbed the last steep pitch to the rim. He had decided there was little chance of running into Bartlett, that only an accident would put the man into their hands. He wondered if he had made a mistake when he'd ridden away from the willows.

Then they tipped over the rim and started across a bench when a rifle cracked. Nolan heard the solid *thwack* of the bullet hitting solid flesh, he saw the flash of gunfire and the burst of powdersmoke and he saw Pony Bartlett partly hidden by the trunk of a quaking asp: all of this in one terrifying second. He clawed for his gun and he dived out of the saddle, knowing that he would be the next man Bartlett would take.

Nolan hit the ground harder than he expected, the fall making him drop his gun and knocking the wind out of him. He thought he heard another shot, but he wasn't sure. He took several agonizing seconds to suck air back into his tortured lungs, his right hand feeling on the ground for his gun, and all the time the terrible fear was in him that Bartlett would fire again and a bullet would smash into him just as it had driven into Kirk Lamm's body.

'Looks like the hunt's finished for Pony Bartlett,' Grant said. 'Lamm, too. He caught that one dead center.'

Nolan got up, still shaky and laboring for breath. He discovered that his gun was in his hand. He looked at Lamm who lay on his back, his arms flung out on both sides of him, blood soaking the front of his shirt. Slowly Nolan walked to where Grant stood staring at Bartlett's body.

'I was downright lucky,' Grant said. 'He was standing sideways back of that quakie. He knowed we was coming up right about here, looks like, but there wasn't no tree big enough right close to hide him. When I fired,

164

I aimed at his head and I got him right through the eye.'

Bartlett had been killed instantly, Nolan thought. He said, 'Seems like a fool play, standing there like that. I saw him the minute he shot, but if I'd stayed on my horse, he'd have drilled me before I could have pulled my gun.' He turned to Grant. 'I guess I heard your shot right after I heard Bartlett's. How'd you get one off so fast?'

Grant gave him a small grin. 'I figured he was up here waiting for us, so when I came up over the rim, I had my gun in my hand. I let go almost the same time he did. Like I said, it was a lucky shot, but if it hadn't been, you'd be dead. I might, too.' He knelt beside the body and went through the pockets, then felt for a money belt. He rose, shaking his head. 'He ain't got the money on him, and he didn't have no saddlebags.'

Grant walked back to his horse, adding, 'No, it wasn't such a fool play, Sheriff. The odds were he could knock off all three of us before we started shooting. Or two of us at least, and he was gambling that whichever one of us was left was a bad shot. That was his mistake. He should of plugged me first.'

Grant was deadly, Nolan thought as he mounted. Strange how you think you know a man for years; you ride with him on posse after posse, but until you face an emergency with him, you don't really know him. Nolan glanced at Lamm's body. The three men who had murdered his son were dead, but Kirk Lamm had not lived long enough to dance on their coffins.

'Where now?' Grant asked. 'Old Hig's cabin?'

'That's right,' Nolan said. 'But we're not pushing till dark. Keep your eyes open for Dillard. That bastard might decide to finish what Bartlett started.'

They reached the road and turned upslope, riding slowly. Grant held his revolver in his right hand, his eyes searching the timber ahead of them. They reached the clearing that held Old Hig's barn and cabin; they stopped and studied the buildings. Except for the smoke lifting from the chimney into the cold air, there was no hint of life around the place.

'Let's put our horses in the barn,' Nolan said. 'We can get them out of the cold anyhow.'

Grant nodded. 'Dillard might be in the cabin with 'em. If he is, we've got trouble.'

They rode across the clearing to the barn and dismounted and led the horses inside, then closed the door. The only animals they found in the barn were Old Hig's riding mare and his pack horse.

'Don't look to me like Dillard's here,' Grant said.

'One of us better keep an eye on the

cabin,' Nolan said worriedly. 'That bastard got under my hide this morning. I guess it was because he fooled me. I figured he didn't amount to much, about Steve Albert's caliber, but I was wrong. I don't want to be surprised by him again.'

'We'll watch it,' Grant said.

The afternoon dragged for Nolan, but Grant gave no indication that the waiting bothered him. He was like an Indian, Nolan thought, with all the patience in the world. He would probably kill Old Hig before he was done. Nolan had had no idea how much Grant hated the old man until they had reached his place and Grant had wanted to work on him, but Nolan knew now, and the knowledge gave him a new worry. Craig would try to make Grant stand trial for the murder of Banjo Smith and Doak Watts. If he added Old Hig to his list, Nolan could not save him.

Nolan waited and smoked and thought. It was the thinking that bothered him. What was there in Harmony to go back to? Criticism for the way he had handled the posse. Defeat the next time he ran for office. The bitter memories that had piled up over the years. The irrigation project gone down the drain. Men like Lee Jameson living on Poverty Flat who had so much reason to kill him that one of them might try.

The coldly logical thing to do was to take

the money if they found it and get out of the county. Just keep going. Sure, he'd have to split it with Grant, but that would leave $25,000, a fortune in Mexico.

He finished his cigarette and rubbed it out, intrigued by the thought and still hating it. He was not aware that it had become night until Grant said, 'Let's go. They won't see us until we're there.'

Nolan opened the barn door, wondering what Grant would say if he made an offer to split the money and get out of the country. It would surprise Grant. He might turn it down, saying he didn't want to ride the owlhoot the rest of his life. Well, they hadn't found the money, but he had a hunch they would, probably in Old Hig's cabin.

They climbed the slope, Nolan discovering that the windows had been covered by blankets. A lamp inside was lighted, but it was impossible to see through the windows. When they reached the porch, Nolan laid a hand on Grant's shoulder. He whispered, 'Listen.'

There was a steady interchange of talk from inside, a woman's voice and then Old Hig's. It struck Nolan that they were arguing about something. The woman raised her voice to say, 'Hig, we haven't seen or heard anything of them for hours, not since they quit shooting. You don't know they're anywhere around here. We've got to have water. If I don't get some, we won't even have coffee in the morning.'

'Damn it, we can do without coffee,' Old Hig snapped. 'You stay inside. If we've got to have water, I'll go get it.'

'You lie right there in bed,' she said.

Nolan heard the bar being lifted, then the door swung open and Laurie Jameson stepped outside. Nolan pinned her hands to her sides before she could say a word. Grant lunged through the door, his revolver in his hand. Old Hig, who had been lying on the bunk, started to get up, then lay back, cursing.

Nolan marched the girl into the cabin. He said, 'Let's make this quick. We haven't found the money, but I'll tell you what we know. The three men who held up the bank are dead. They didn't have the money. They wouldn't have been hanging around here in the Catclaws if they'd had it. That leaves you. Where is it?'

'Don't say a word, Laurie,' Old Hig yelled. 'These devils will kill both of us if you tell 'em anything.'

The girl struggled to break out of Nolan's grip, but she could not. She said nothing, her lips pressed so tightly together they were white. Nolan didn't like the notion of torturing her to make her talk, but that might be the only way they could get the information from her.

169

Grant walked toward the bunk. He said, 'Change her mind, old man, or we'll work you over to a frazzle.'

'No,' Laurie screamed. 'Morgan Dillard's around here. He'll kill you if you do anything to Old Hig.'

'He's a little slow getting here.' Grant caught the old man by the shoulder and lifted him off the bunk. 'Where's the money?'

'I don't know...' Old Hig began.

Grant hit him on the side of the head. Nolan said to Laurie, 'You'd better tell us what we want to know. Grant hates the old man. He'll kill him if you don't talk.'

'You're an animal,' Laurie cried. 'You hurt him when you beat him up before.'

Grant hit Higgins again, rocking the old man's head. Laurie whimpered, 'All right, I'll tell you. Don't hurt him any more.'

'No,' Old Hig shouted. 'Don't...'

'It's in the barn,' Laurie said. 'I buried it that night after the holdup. It's in the back stall about six feet from the manger.'

'Let's go see, Zach,' Nolan said. 'If you're lying, God help you.'

Nolan picked up Old Hig's rifle, the only gun in the cabin. He ran down the slope behind Grant who was the first to enter the barn. Nolan pulled the door shut as Grant lighted a lantern that hung from a peg, picked up a fork, and scraped the litter away from the floor of the back stall. He prodded until the prongs of the fork struck soft dirt, then he began to dig. He found three sacks within a minute or so and stepped back, panting.

'Here they are, Sheriff,' Grant said. 'See if the money's in 'em.'

Nolan knelt beside the hole and opened the sacks. He said, 'Yeah, looks like it's here.'

'Fine,' Grant said in a low tone. 'Get up, Sheriff. Walk back along the runway. I don't like to shoot a man when he's on his knees.'

Nolan froze. He didn't look at Grant. He didn't need to. There wasn't the slightest doubt in his mind about Grant's intentions. The thought occurred to him that he had considered offering Grant an even split, but with him it was all or nothing.

'We're a posse, Zach,' Nolan said. 'We're not outlaws stealing the bank's money.'

'I'll be an outlaw after tonight either way I jump,' Grant said. 'You think I'm going back to Harmony and let 'em string me up because I helped Lamm hang Smith and Watts? Now you get up and start walking.'

Slowly Nolan got to his feet and backed out of the stall. He must be having a nightmare, he thought, the worst nightmare he'd ever had. He wasn't going to wake up from this one.

CHAPTER NINETEEN

Morgan rode as hard as he could, dismounting at times and running beside his sorrel. He was afraid, more afraid than he had ever been in his life before. Old Hig, already sick from the beating the posse had given him, could not hold out against men as brutal as Nolan and Grant and Lamm.

Even if Laurie succeeded in hiding in the hole under the trap door, Nolan and the others would torture the old man until he told them where they would find Laurie. Once they had their hands on her ...

He could not bring himself to even think of that. It wasn't just that Laurie was a fine, decent girl. She had come to mean something to him these last hours, something he had dreamed Mamie Albert would mean, but never had.

The canyon walls became steeper and higher as he climbed toward the summit, blotting out most of the sunlight so that the road which followed the stream in the bottom of the canyon was in twilight long before the sun was down.

All the time Morgan cursed himself for taking Laurie to Old Hig's cabin. She would have been better off to have ridden with him, but that was something he could not have known. If she had stayed with him and he had been forced into a fight, she would have been in danger. Either way it was a calculated gamble, and he had taken the course that seemed to offer her the greater safety.

The point where he had made his mistake was in not thinking the posse would look for her at Old Hig's cabin. They had doubtless returned to his ranch after failing to find the outlaws in Bardo; they had searched his buildings and then had gone to Alberts' where Steve had told them what they suspected about Laurie and that she had left with Morgan. After that Nolan's thinking must have paralleled Morgan's. By the process of elimination he would decide Old Hig's cabin was the logical place for her to go.

By the time Morgan reached the park where the north and south forks of Smoky river came together, the last of the thin dusk light had faded into darkness. He dug in his spurs now, the open ground leveling off toward the summit, Old Hig's buildings were directly ahead.

He started angling toward the cabin which was on the crest of the divide, then noticed there was a light in the barn. He turned his gelding toward the barn, not sure why he made this split-second decision except that he had not expected to find a light in the barn. He had better see about it, he thought, before he went on to the house.

Old Hig and Laurie were smart enough to stay inside the cabin and keep the door barred, so neither of them should be down here in the barn. Morgan didn't know what to expect as he reined his horse to a stop and drew his gun, but the fear that had been in him all the way up Smoky river now became intolerable.

The one possibility that had worried him from the moment he had left Harmony was that through some trick or threat, Nolan and the others had got into the cabin and had found Laurie. They might have her in the barn now.

Morgan put his hand on the door to pull it open when he heard Nolan cry out as if in agony, 'Don't do it, Zach. We've always been friends.'

'Friends?' It was Grant's voice, cold and contemptuous. 'Friends when you needed a man to go with a posse, a man who could track and shoot and a man you knew you could depend on in a fight, but on any other day I wasn't worth your notice. I was just an odd job man around town who could be hired to spade a garden or move a privy or clean a chicken pen or fork out a stable.'

'It wasn't that...'

'Shut up,' Grant said. 'For once in my life I've got a fortune just waiting to be taken. I ain't gonna pass it up, and you've got enough sense to know I can't leave you alive. Now, by God, I'm heading for Mexico, and I'll be there by the time they find somebody else fool enough to wear their star.'

Morgan thumbed back the hammer of his Colt as he yanked the door open. He heard the crashing sound of Grant's revolver and he saw Nolan, standing in the runway behind the stalls, go down. Grant threw a shot at Morgan. He felt the breath of the bullet against his cheek as he fired, then he paced slowly toward Grant, his cocked .45 in his hand.

Grant was slammed back against the wall by the heavy slug, an expression of blank shock on his lean, sun-burned face. He still held to his gun that dangled at his side. He tried to lift it, but he lacked the strength. Life was flowing out of him as blood spread across his shirt.

'Nolan said you was the man ... to ... watch,' Grant whispered.

Grant's feet slid out from under him and he sat down in the litter on the barn floor, his shoulders and head braced against the wall. For a moment he remained that way, his wide, blank eyes on Morgan, then he fell sideways. Morgan knelt beside him and felt for his pulse. There was none.

Morgan turned to Nolan. The sheriff was holding his left leg, blood staining his pants above the knee. 'He could have killed me as easy as shooting me in the leg,' Nolan muttered. 'He aimed to beef me slow so it would hurt and I'd beg for my life. He hated me just like he hated Old Hig, but I never guessed.'

Quickly Morgan took out his knife and slit Nolan's pant's leg. The bullet had gone through the flesh, but had not touched the bone. Morgan said, 'I'll help you up and you can get on my horse if you think you can ride as far as the cabin.'

'I'll come nearer riding than walking,' Nolan grated.

Morgan helped him out of the barn and into the saddle. He sat there gripping the horn, cursing and groaning until Morgan asked, 'Where's the money?'

'In the back stall,' Nolan said. 'Hurry up and get me into bed before I bleed to death.'

Morgan found the sacks where Nolan said they were. Returning to the sorrel, he took the reins and led the horse to the cabin, Nolan still hanging to the horn with both hands. Morgan called, 'Laurie! Hig! Open up. It's me, Morgan.'

Laurie lifted the bar and opened the door. She ran onto the porch and threw herself into Morgan's arms. She hugged him, then looked up at him, the lamplight falling through the open door onto her face.

'Is it over?' she asked. 'Is it really over?'

'Grant's dead and I've got the money.' Morgan turned to Nolan. 'Where's Lamm?'

'Bartlett shot him and Grant shot Bartlett,' Nolan said. 'Now get me inside, will you?'

Morgan helped him to the ground and across the porch and into the cabin. Old Hig sat on the bunk, and when he saw Nolan, he laughed. He said, 'Well now, Sheriff, the shoe's on the other foot, ain't it? You want my bunk, do you? Well sir, you let Grant beat the tar out of me and now I don't feel like sitting up.'

'Then put me on the floor,' Nolan groaned. 'I've got to get off this leg. Go after Doc Vance, will you, Dillard?'

'Sure, I'll go,' Morgan said, 'and Laurie's going with me. I'll let Old Hig bandage that bullet hole.'

The old man got up, still laughing. 'Yes, sir, the shoe is sure on the other foot. I'll be glad to bandage his bullet hole, Dillard. Is that water boiling, Laurie?'

'Yes, it's boiling,' Laurie answered.

'Good.' Old Hig snickered. 'There's nothing that'll cure a bullet wound faster'n pouring boiling water on it. Makes a man forget how much the bullet hole hurts. Here, Nolan, you're worse off'n I am. You lie down while I get the boiling water. The Lord delivered you into my hands.'

'Dillard, don't leave me with this old

177

bastard,' Nolan screamed. 'He'll kill me.'

'Yeah, he sure might,' Morgan agreed. 'Before Laurie and I go, there's a thing or two we'd better talk over. I just came from Harmony where me'n Craig and Vance kind of settled things. They took my offer, the money back for the water being turned into the Dry Fork canal. You were a partner in that irrigation company. I don't know how they can open the bank without Kirk Lamm, but that's not my worry. Enforcing the law might be. Craig was talking about having me appointed sheriff. What are your plans?'

Nolan lay on his back, his fists clenched. 'There's nothing to hold me here if that's what you're getting at. I'm pulling out and starting somewhere else as soon as I'm able to ride. You can have the damned star.' He bit his lower lip to hold back a groan, then he added, 'I knew you were bad medicine this morning, but you saved my life at that.'

'Get your coat,' Morgan told Laurie. 'You need to get home. Your pa's been hurt. The posse beat him up.'

Laurie slipped into her coat, then she stood beside the bunk looking at Nolan, her lips curling in contempt. 'It's time for honest law in this county. I guess it's even a little past time.'

She walked out of the cabin and down the slope toward the barn, Morgan leading his sorrel and striding along beside her. They reached the barn before she could speak, then she said, 'I think I would have killed him if I'd stayed, Morgan. They were such brutes, Nolan and Grant.'

'Lamm, too,' Morgan said, thinking of the boys Lamm and Grant had lynched. 'One thing, Laurie. Don't mention to anyone that you had a part in the bank robbery. Craig and the rest won't ask any questions. All they want is the money.'

She looked up at him, smiling a little. 'All we want is the water, but it will take time and work to bring the Dry Fork country back. Will you help?'

'Sure I'll help,' he answered. 'I don't see any future for me on Peace Creek.' He hesitated, then added, 'You think we might have a future on the Dry Fork?'

'Of course we do,' she said. 'Now, will you saddle Old Hig's mare for me?'

As he went into the barn, he hoped he never found another girl in his haystack. This one was going to last him a lifetime.

Wayne D. Overholser has won three Golden Spur awards from the Western Writers of America and has a long list of fine Western titles to his credit. He was born in Pomeroy, Washington, and attended the University of Montana, University of Oregon, and the University of Southern California before becoming a public school teacher and principal in various Oregon communities. He began writing for Western pulp magazines in 1936 and within a couple of years was a regular contributor to Street and Smith's WESTERN STORY and Fiction House's LARIAT STORY MAGAZINE. BUCKAROO'S CODE (1984) was his first Western novel and still one of his best. In the 1950s and 1960s, having retired from academic work to concentrate on writing, he would publish as many as four books a year under his own name or a pseudonym, most prominently as Joseph Wayne. THE BITTER NIGHT, THE LONE DEPUTY, and THE VIOLENT LAND are among the finest of the early Overholser titles. He was asked by William MacLeod Raine, that dean among Western writers, to complete his last novel after Raine's death. Some of Overholser's most rewarding novels were actually collaborations with other Western writers, COLORADO GOLD with Chad Merriman and SHOWDOWN AT STONY CREEK with Lewis B. Patten. Overholser's Western novels, no matter under what name they have been published, are based on a solid knowledge of the history and customs of the nineteenth-century West, particularly when set in his two favorite Western states, Oregon and Colorado. Many of his novels are first person narratives, a technique that tends to bring an added dimension of vividness to the frontier experiences of his narrators and frequently, as in CAST A LONG SHADOW, the female characters one encounters are among the most memorable. He has written his numerous novels with a consistent skill and an uncommon sensitivity to the depths of human character. Almost invariably, his stories weave a spell of their own with their scenes and images of social and economic forces often in conflict and the diverse ways of life and personalities that made the American Western frontier so unique a time and place in human history.